FLOOD WORLD

TOM HUDDLESTON

nosy
crow

First published in the UK in 2019 by Nosy Crow Ltd
The Crow's Nest, 14 Baden Place
Crosby Row, London, SE1 1YW

Nosy Crow and associated logos are trademarks and/or registered
trademarks of Nosy Crow Ltd

3 5 7 9 10 8 6 4

A CIP catalogue record for this book is available from the
British Library.

Printed and bound in Great Britain by Clays Ltd, Elcograf S.p.A.
Typeset by Tiger Media

Papers used by Nosy Crow are made from wood grown in
sustainable forests

ISBN: 978 1 78800 434 3

www.nosycrow.com

For Pat & Kat

"I would not creep along the coast but steer
Out in mid-sea, by guidance of the stars."

George Eliot

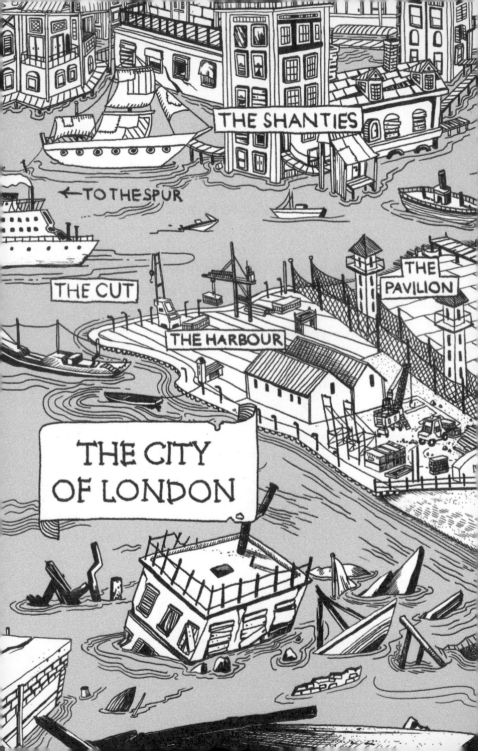

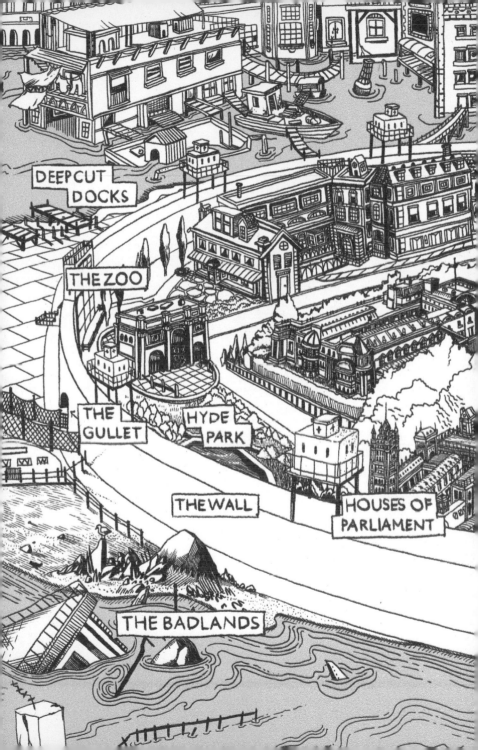

1

The City and the Sea

Joe skidded to a stop, breaking from the shadow of the buildings to stand in wonder at the water's edge. Ahead of him the filthy brown sea met the cloudless blue sky. In the distance a line of tower blocks jutted from the water, waves lapping at the middlemost storeys.

"Hey!" Kara called. "Don't run ahead." Her bare feet pounded on the wooden walkway as she came up behind him, her face flushed and her dirty yellow hair coming loose from its knot.

"I wanted to see the boats," Joe said. "I like the boats."

The Cut was busy today, the shipping lanes crowded with rusted tankers and boxy haulers, some creeping into port while others rattled off towards open water and destinations unknown. Local fishing sloops tacked between them, patchwork sails stiffening in the breeze.

All of them were going somewhere. Somewhere that wasn't here.

"It's dangerous out this way, you know that." Kara placed a protective arm round his shoulders. "We're a long way from home."

She was right, as usual. The Spur was the most notorious neighbourhood in the Shanties, an outflung tangle of wooden catwalks, shadowy towers and winding waterways miles from the heart of things. Only the very poor or very secretive made their homes out here.

"This ain't a race, you know," a voice called, and turning back Joe saw Mr Colpeper struggling behind them, his bald head scarlet and glistening. Far beyond him the Wall rose from the concrete and driftwood sprawl of the Shanties, its sloping side sparkling with a layer of crystal salt. At its base was the harbour, a busy ant's nest prickling with cranes and masts and security towers.

Colpeper wheezed to a halt, his hands on his knees. "You kids'll be the death of me, I swear."

"You're getting fat," Kara said. "What? It's true."

Colpeper's mouth tightened, then he barked a bitter laugh. "You don't mince words, do you, sweetheart? One of these days that mouth'll get you into trouble."

He hitched up his jeans, staring out along the Spur. A short distance ahead the walkway tapered to its end, the blocks petering out into a rickety huddle of rafts and shacks. Beyond that there was nothing but open ocean.

"Past the pub then look for the spire, my dealer said." Colpeper rubbed his hands. "He's already got a buyer lined up in the City. This could be it for us, kids. Top dollar, right in our pockets."

"Where have I heard that before?" Kara muttered sceptically. Colpeper was always sure this job was the big one, the chance of a lifetime. But somehow it never quite panned out.

Waves lapped at the concrete pilings as they moved along the walkway. An old man perched on the edge, clasping a homemade fishing rod. *What's he expecting to catch?* Joe wondered. *Rusty cans and bleached bones.* Perhaps he was one of the ancient ones, who remembered London before the last barrier broke. Who'd lost everything to the waves.

Joe had tried to imagine a life on dry land, but he was never quite able to grasp it. Solid earth under your feet and all that green stuff – what did they call it, grass? The Shanties might be smelly and hectic and dangerous, but this was the only world he'd ever known.

Well, that wasn't strictly true. He'd been to another world, one that few ever got to see. And it was almost time to go back.

"Keep up," Kara called over her shoulder. "Honestly, first you run off, now you're stood there daydreaming."

She reached out and he took her hand, enjoying as he always did the sight of his little brown paw clasped in her big rosy-pink one. She tugged him forward, resentfully at first, then with a smile. "You are such a pain in the bum," she laughed. "I don't know why I let you hang around with me."

"Because you lurve me," Joe told her. "You lurve me so much, it's disgusting."

Kara lowered her head and kept dragging. "Horrid. Little. Brat," she grunted with each tug.

"Quiet, you two," Colpeper said abruptly. "This isn't the place for games."

A rusty shack loomed ahead, casting the walkway into shadow. The raft beneath it rocked in the wake of a passing ship and the whole structure creaked and groaned. Through the open door Joe could see figures moving through a fog of sweet smoke. He heard the clink of glasses and smelled the sour tang of a strong, locally brewed drink folks called Selkie.

"This is the Last Gasp," Colpeper whispered. "Only the really bad crooks drink in here."

"Favourite of yours, then?" Kara smirked.

Colpeper nodded. "It was, back in the day. Before

I went legit. You're lucky you didn't know me then, I wasn't half so good-natured."

His voice was almost wistful, and Joe wondered how much Mr Colpeper had really changed. He was decent enough most of the time, but when he got in one of his tempers no Beef would dare stand up to him.

They passed the pub, approaching the tip of the Spur. Squinting ahead, Joe realised this might be the furthest from home he'd ever been. Across the water he could make out a smudge on the horizon – the hazy mainland shores of Wycombe and the Chilterns, so distant and unattainable he might as well have been gazing at the moon.

"That must be the spire," the big man said, gesturing south into the waters of the Cut. The peak of a building broke the surface, topped with the outline of a black bird. Joe peeled off his shirt and Colpeper unzipped his pack, taking out a rubber mask and a steel canister. "Just take a look for now. If the goods are intact, we'll see about proper salvage."

Joe nodded, clipping the tank to his cargo shorts and biting down on the mouthpiece. The oxygen tasted of old rust.

"And don't take any stupid risks," Kara warned him. "It's not worth it."

Joe frowned. "I hab dud dis befaw, oo no," he told her, the mouthpiece garbling his words. It was good that she worried, but sometimes he wished she'd put a bit more trust in him.

He dropped to the boards, flippers dangling over the edge. Scum glistened on the water, a seagull carcass grinning from a nest of seaweed. The Stain, they called it, a festering vortex of garbage and human waste that spread from the Shanties for miles in every direction. But he had no choice; they'd come all this way. So he braced himself and took the plunge.

Joe trod water, taking a good look left and right. He wasn't close enough to the sea lanes to worry about the big ships, but it'd be just his luck if some idiot on a jetski came clipping round the corner. Then he kicked out, beating a path through the muck, keeping his arms and legs tucked in to limit the risk of touching anything unpleasant. He kept his scalp shaved for the same reason; there was nothing worse than washing someone else's poo out of your hair.

He reached the spire, the sun baking on his back. He gave a thumbs up, receiving an answering nod from Colpeper. Then he kicked off, angling down into the dark. The Stain cleared, a shaft of sunlight broke through and the world below was revealed.

The houses here were low, a maze of narrow terraces and algae-stained roofs. Joe saw shattered windows, rotting curtains waving in the current. But there were no cars – they must've been dragged up for scrap years ago, along with anything else the early Beefs had seen fit to scavenge. This whole area had been picked clean.

He thought of the old fisherman. Had he grown up in a street like this, before the water came? Decades had passed since then, but time had no meaning down here.

Joe turned, treading water and looking up at the building looming over him. A church, Colpeper had called it. He knew what the word meant; the Shanties were full of shacks where the faithful gathered to sing and pray. Kara had always cautioned him to steer clear – if there is a god, she said, he's probably not someone you want to make friends with. I mean, look at the world.

But this church was different and rather grand. From the corners of the steeple sprouted four stone carvings, horned figures with spread wings. They looked oddly at home down here, watching over their sunken kingdom.

Joe scanned the nearby buildings for the word Colpeper had made him memorise. A sign said POST OFFICE, another SUPERMARKET – a large flat structure with a line of rusty carts anchored outside. Then he saw it. Letters were missing so that the sign now read "R XY C EMA", but this had to be the place. It was a squat brick building, the entrance just a gaping rust-edged hole. Joe swam closer, taking hold of the steel frame. He peered inside.

The carpets, once red, were almost black with silt. Joe tugged the torch from his pocket, winding the crank five times, then flicking the switch. Shapes emerged from the gloom: rotted chairs and a smooth fibreglass counter. The walls were lined with pictures sealed in grimy frames. Joe wiped one clean and saw a woman wearing next to nothing holding a gun in her hand. He wondered what kind of place it had been, this cinema.

Silver winked as a school of sprats darted out of the light. Doors branched left and right, blocked with fallen debris. But in the far corner a flight of steps led up to another larger door. A sign read SCREEN ONE just like Colpeper said.

The hinges were stiff but a few cautious tugs pulled the door wide enough for Joe to squeeze through. The room inside was dark and cavernous. He felt his heartbeat quicken. It wouldn't take much, a rotted roof beam or a rusted girder, and he'd be trapped, crushed in the rubble or buried alive until his air ran out. It wasn't uncommon these days; with each passing year they had to swim deeper and search harder to find anything worth bringing up. The life of a Beef was getting riskier all the time.

The room was full of chairs all facing the opposite way. The far wall was perfectly flat and perfectly white, and Joe wondered why people would come in here to sit and stare at nothing. Perhaps this was another sort of church – maybe they'd flash pictures of their god on that wall and sing hymns in the dark.

Something brushed against Joe's foot and he started. A sea snake wound into the darkness, undulating bands of yellow and black. He took a deep pull of oxygen. This place was starting to give him the creeps.

A glint of reflected light told him he'd found what he was looking for. A glass case stood against the wall, a laminated sign taped to it. The words were faded but readable: COLLECT 10 TOKENS TO CLAIM YOUR EXCLUSIVE ACTION FIGURE!

He peered closer and his heart sank. A jagged crack ran across the face of the cabinet and the inside was full of filthy water. Colpeper had been very clear – any damage and the sale would be off. Joe spat out his mouthpiece, clasping the torch between his teeth. He touched the front of the case and the glass fell away, the hinges rusted to nothing. The objects inside were soaked but he reached in anyway, fingers wrapping round something small and hard.

It looked like a sort of skinny bear standing on two feet. His fur had once been brown but the paint had soaked away to reveal textured grey plastic underneath. His lips were drawn back in a snarl, but his eyes were still blue and there was something friendly about him. Joe scratched the bear under the chin and pondered.

So this was what he had been sent to find. Plastic toys, the kind they kept in a crate at school for the younger kids to play with. And yet someone inside the City – a collector, Colpeper had called him – was willing to pay serious money for them. Maybe this collector didn't know that someone like Joe would end up risking his life to get them. Maybe he didn't know that the money he'd offered could keep a Shanty family alive for a year. Or maybe he just didn't care.

Joe slipped the plastic figure into his pocket, reaching for his mouthpiece. But as he did so something scraped against his arm and he jerked round in surprise. Empty eye sockets stared back, white teeth grinning from a face picked clean.

The air exploded from Joe's lungs, the torch slipping from between his teeth. It tumbled down into the silt and the room was plunged into darkness.

Joe scrabbled for his mouthpiece, hands shaking. He felt the skeleton drift alongside, bony fingers scraping at his scalp. He'd seen bodies before, human and animal, that was just part of being a Beef. But he'd never been touched by one before.

He found the mouthpiece and shoved it in, taking an urgent breath. The torch glimmered below him and he scrabbled for it, taking hold just as the bulb died. *Lucky*, he thought. A few more seconds and he might never have found it.

He wound the crank, the beam flashing across white bone. He shut his eyes and gave a shove. Limbs spun loose, ribs and vertebrae tumbling into the darkness.

He wiped his hands on his shorts, knowing it was a ridiculous thing to do. He almost laughed, then he gathered himself. The only thing left was to head back up and break the news to his boss. Hopefully Colpeper was in a forgiving mood.

2

The Chase

Kara stood on the walkway staring down into the water. Doubt tugged at her heart; it was the same each time Joe went under. She knew she was being soft, that he knew what he was doing. But they'd known two kids this year, good hard-working Beefs, who simply hadn't surfaced. And she didn't know what she'd do if she lost Joe.

Colpeper sat, letting his hairy legs dangle over the side. Sweat pooled in the folds of his neck. "You worry about him," he said. "He's lucky."

Kara frowned. "Lucky how?"

"Lucky to have a big sister looking out for him."

"I'm not his sister," Kara said. "And if I was any good at looking after him he wouldn't be risking his neck for a few measly quid."

Colpeper grunted. "Don't be so hard on yourself.

In the Shanties you either work or you starve; it's not your fault Joe's skills are more valuable right now than yours."

Kara frowned. "What skills? I don't have any skills."

"Come on," Colpeper grinned. "You can hot-wire a speedboat faster than anyone I ever met."

"I don't do that any more," Kara said. "Not after last time. That docker would've killed me if he'd caught me."

Colpeper struggled to his feet. "I've actually been meaning to have a word with you. I've a prospect on the horizon. I know, you've heard it before. But this one could be the answer to all our problems." He was trying to seem casual, but Kara could hear the edge in his voice. She'd heard rumours that Colpeper owed big money to bad people, that he'd borrowed from the Shore Boys and couldn't cover his payments.

"A certain acquaintance has tipped me off about a few possibilities," he went on. "Shipping, import-export, that sort of thing."

"You mean smuggling," Kara said. "Smuggling what?"

Colpeper shifted uncomfortably. "Well, you know, protective devices. Defensive supplies."

Kara's eyebrows shot up. "You're going to run guns? And you want us to help you?"

"Not the boy," Colpeper said quickly. "Not till he's older. But look, I know you don't like hearing it but you're a smart girl, Kara. Nothing gets past you. And you're tougher than you look; people always underestimate you. You're perfect for this gig. The Beef work's drying up, and you know what the alternatives are for kids your age in a place like this."

Kara sighed. He had a point. "So where would we acquire these ... defensive supplies?"

Colpeper flushed. "Judging from my friend's sympathies, I guess they'd come from the Mariners."

Kara's mouth dropped open. "But the Mariners are terrorists! They've killed our people, boarded our ships..."

"What d'you mean, *our*?" Colpeper asked. "Maybe they raid the odd trading vessel but that's no skin off your nose, is it? Have they ever hurt anyone in the Shanties?"

"What about that warehouse explosion in the Hackney Sink?" Kara asked. "Fifteen people died. The newsfeeds said it could've been ordered by John Cortez himself."

Colpeper laughed. "I happen to know what was going on in that warehouse, and it involved a lot of unstable chemicals. The newsfeeds blame the Mariners cos it makes for a good story, and the government encourage it because it distracts poor Shanty rats like us from our real problems. But the Mariners make the best weapons, the kind you hardly ever see on the market. I can't pass this up."

"But they're freaks," Kara complained. "They don't even have proper homes; they just float around in those weird Arks of theirs. And they eat seaweed!"

"I eat seaweed. It's full of nutrients."

Kara humphed. "Not for every meal." She didn't like the thought of smuggling guns, not from a bunch of seaweed-eating terrorists. But what choice did she have? Someone else would take her place if she turned Colpeper down, and someone else would get the money.

She unhooked a water bottle from her waistband, emptying the dregs into her mouth. The taste of san-sal formula made her gag.

"Where is that boy?" Colpeper asked, looking at his comwatch. "Shouldn't take forever to…"

A sound tore the air, a shuddering blast echoing from the sunken towers. Kara spun, shielding her eyes. In the distance, below the Wall, a column of black smoke was rising.

Gunfire rattled in the stillness and out in the Cut something moved, weaving between the big ships. Kara saw a fast-moving blur, darting under anchor chains and bowlines, heading for the open sea. The silver jetski carried a single passenger, upright in the saddle. He wore dockers' overalls, brown over white, and as he curved round the rust-pocked prow of a tanker he turned back, taking aim. Three distant pops sounded over the water, then he revved the throttle and the ski picked up speed, thundering out into the harbour.

Now Kara could see what he'd been shooting at. A MetCo gunboat came slicing through the shallows, riding low and fast, gushing chemical smoke. Uniformed cops huddled behind the plastiglass rear-gun seat. One of them strapped himself into the rear gunseat, kicking at the controls. The twin barrels spun and rose, training on the fleeing jetski, compensating for the bucking of the speedboat as it rocketed through the water.

There was a roar and the cannons spat blue fire. The jetski twisted just in time, banking violently, sending up a wall of spray. The firebolt hit the water, plumes of steam rising.

The rider scanned the Spur desperately, looking for any route back into the Shanties. He angled towards the Last Gasp, where a wooden jetty branched out into the Cut. Beside it the pilings parted, forming a low bridge. If he ducked, he might make it.

The ski drew closer, and closer still. Kara could hear the whine of the propeller, could see fear in the rider's eyes.

Then she saw another shape, low in the water, right in the jetski's path. A dark brown head broke the surface and she cried out in horror.

Joe spat out his mouthpiece, gulping real air. He swallowed, and as his ears popped he heard the roar of an approaching engine. He twisted, trying to take his bearings.

His breath stopped. The jetski was less than fifty feet away and coming fast. There was no time to swim clear, and if he tried to duck the propeller would slice his head open. He felt his bladder go, warmth on his legs.

Then the rider saw him, and for the briefest moment their eyes locked. He was a young man, thin and bearded, his eyes widening in panic. He glanced up at the Spur and the choice was plain – hold his course and end Joe's life, or turn aside and risk his own. He gripped the bars as the ski closed in, twenty feet, now ten. Joe bit his tongue and waited to die.

At the last second the young man tugged on the steering bar and the ski slalomed sideways. Joe felt the wind of the propeller as it missed him by inches, the ski gliding on the glassy surface of the water. It spun once, twice, then it hammered into the jetty behind the Last Gasp and exploded. The rider was thrown free, slamming into the boards, his uniform ablaze.

Joe swam as hard as he could. The jetty had been split almost in two, staves splayed and planks uprooted. The ski lay upended, the propeller chewing angrily at the air. Joe pulled himself from the water, kicking off his flippers. He tasted smoke and chem fumes.

The rider had rolled on his back, dousing the flames. Now he lay still, his eyes wide and sightless, his face scorched and spattered with blood. Joe ran to him, dropping to his knees.

"I'll get help."

But the rider coughed weakly, reaching to take Joe's hand. He was younger than Joe had expected, his scruffy beard barely grown in. His uniform was burned black, the skin beneath blistered. Their eyes met and Joe could see fear in them, and pain, and courage. He wanted to tell him it would be OK, but he didn't think it was true.

"I'm s-sorry…" the dying man wheezed, blood coursing from both sides of his mouth. "I'm so s-sorry…"

Joe squeezed his hand. "Don't be sorry. You saved me."

Then he heard a shout, and looked up.

"Get away from him!" Kara flung herself on to the shattered jetty. "Joe, run to me."

"No," Joe protested. "He's hurt."

But the rider had let go, rolling over on blistered elbows. He began to drag himself forward, summoning the last of his strength to claw his way across the jetty. Colpeper hurried towards them, panting.

Kara ran to Joe's side, clasping him in her arms. "Are you OK?" she demanded. "Did he hurt you?"

Joe shook his head. "He saved my life. We have to call a medic."

"No point," Colpeper said. "He's done for."

The man struggled to the edge of the platform, leaving a trail of blood. He glanced back and Kara saw a look pass between him and Joe, sudden and quiet. Then the stranger gave a last push and toppled face first into the water, sinking like a stone. There was a trail of bubbles and for a moment the grey water blossomed red. Then he was gone.

Joe looked up, tears cutting through the filth on his face. "Why did he do that? We could've helped him."

"He was a Mariner," Colpeper said softly. "He's gone back to the ocean."

Kara looked up. "But I thought you said the Mariners never attacked the Shanties?"

Colpeper frowned. "Seems I spoke too soon."

Kara heard engines idling as the MetCo craft drew closer. Through the smoke she saw an officer upright in the driver's seat, gesturing at them. He had dark eyes and a black moustache.

"You three," he said through a loudhailer. "Don't move."

3

London Zoo

"Try to see it from my side."

The policeman smoothed his moustache, silhouetted in the sunlight streaming through his office window. "A Mariner terrorist is apprehended near the harbour. There's an explosion. He flees, we give chase, but the only person to make actual contact with him is this boy. Is it just a coincidence that he happened to be in precisely the right place at precisely the right time?"

"Do we look like terrorists to you?" Kara shot back, her arm round Joe's shoulders.

The cop shrugged. "If this job's taught me anything, it's that they come in all shapes and sizes."

"And what is your job exactly? Officer in charge of scaring kids?"

The policeman glowered, gesturing to a silver badge

on his shirt. "Akharee Singh, second lieutenant, London Metropolitan Police Corporation. Currently assigned to the Mariner Task Force, which means I hunt terrorists for a living. So don't get smart with me."

Kara bit her tongue. He was right, shooting her mouth off could only get them into more trouble. They were deep in enemy territory here, inside the Wall itself, in the concrete maze of offices, barracks and prison cells where MetCo had their headquarters. Precinct Place was its official title, but everyone called it London Zoo.

Singh's office was unimpressive, a cramped square box with a desk, three chairs and a framed portrait of a man Kara half recognised. But the view from the window was spectacular – over the lieutenant's shoulder she could see right across the Pavilion to the harbour and the towers beyond, their silhouettes stark against the sinking sun.

The Shanties were one big accident, Kara knew – the Wall had been built to keep the rich folks in the City safe when the waters rose, but they hadn't stopped to think who'd cook their food and clean their houses. And so, in the upper floors of submerged blocks and the ramshackle walkways that linked them, the Shanties had sprung up almost overnight. To some it might seem strange, she thought, this floating slum clinging to the outside of the Wall. But to her it was just home.

"Let's try this again," Singh said, making an effort to smile. "Be straight with me, and I'll do the same. What were the two of you doing so far out on the Spur?"

Kara flushed. "We were…"

"Sightseeing," Joe broke in. "Looking at … stuff."

Singh frowned at him. "Sightseeing, in the most dangerous part of the Shanties. And this Colpeper, what was he? Tour guide? Ice-cream man? I don't suppose he's any relation to the Frances Colpeper we picked up last year for running an illegal salvage operation using child labour?"

Kara gulped. "We wouldn't know anything about that."

Singh sighed. "Employing Beefs isn't just an offence for the men who run the gangs. The kids can find themselves in serious trouble too. A night in the cells, a tracker bracelet, even a trip to the work farms if they're really unlucky."

"Well, isn't that just child labour as well?" Kara shot back before she could stop herself.

The lieutenant raised an eyebrow. "I warned you once."

He tapped the touchscreen set into his desk, squinting. "Says here you're Kara Jordan, fifteen years old, father a market trader, knifed in a robbery. Mother died three months later, ruled as suicide."

"It was an accident," Kara said. "She slipped."

Sympathy flickered in Singh's eyes. "You were picked up by the authorities and spent four years at the Sisterhood—"

"I won't go back there," Kara said quickly. "You can't make me."

"Calm, girl. I'm just getting my facts straight. But there's no record of the boy at all. How old is he, eleven? Where are his parents?"

"They ran off," Joe said. "They didn't want me."

"So we're orphans," Kara said. "What are you going to do, adopt us?"

The officer smiled despite himself. "No, but the state could. I could make a few calls, have you placed in care. It'd be a shame if you never got to see each other again."

Kara's chest tightened. These weren't empty threats; Singh had the power to do exactly as he promised. But he could also let them go, drop them back in the Shanties and forget all about them.

"So tell me," he said, leaning forward. "The truth this time. The boy's a bottom feeder, am I right? A Beef? And this Colpeper, he's your crew boss?"

Kara hung her head and nodded.

"But your being out there had nothing to do with the Mariners, did it?"

She looked up. Singh's stare was intense, but there was no suspicion left in it.

"I told you," Kara said. "It just… happened."

The officer settled back. "I believe you. Call me a sucker, but—"

"*What is the meaning of this?*"

The door slammed open and a stocky, barrel-chested man came shouldering in, his face as red as a marker buoy. "Explain yourself, second lieutenant." He wore a sharp black suit with the MetCo logo on the breast, and his light brown hair clung to his head like a shaggy animal. Kara glanced up at the portrait on the wall; it was the same man, and now she remembered his name: Alexander Remick, CEO of MetCo and head of security for the whole of London.

Singh blanched. "Sir, I didn't… I had no…"

"Clearly not," Remick growled. "We have a major incident on our hands and I find you tucked up indoors, chatting with a pair of filthy mudlarks. Let me assure you, minister, this is not how I train my officers to behave."

Kara craned her neck, seeing a tall, serious-looking woman standing behind him in the corridor. She wore a grey skirt and carried a leather briefcase printed with the symbol of the crown. A government minister, Kara realised. Here in the Shanties. This must be serious.

Singh saw her too, and his jaw tightened. "Th-these are the witnesses from my report," he stammered. "They were on site when the Mariner went into the water. The lad even spoke to him."

Remick regarded them with icy interest. Joe stuck his hand out, but Remick just stared at it until he put it away again. "Well, young man? What did the terrorist have to say?"

Joe gulped. "H-he said he was s-sorry. I tried to h-help him, and he died."

"Is it your habit to offer aid to insurgents?" Remick asked, leaning closer. "Are you a friend to the Mariners, boy?"

"No," Joe squeaked. "I didn't… He wasn't…"

"He didn't have a shirt with Mariner written on it," Kara said. "How was Joe meant to know?"

Remick's face darkened. "He was being pursued by my men. That ought to be enough." He forced a smile, turning back to the woman. "My apologies for this slight delay, my dear minister. I just need a moment with my subordinate, so if you wouldn't mind waiting down at the front desk we'll have this squared away in no time."

The minister smiled thinly. "Very well, Mr Remick. But please don't dawdle; we have a lot to attend to."

Remick closed the door softly, then he turned on

27

Singh, nostrils flaring. "Do you know who that was? No? I'll enlighten you. Her name is Patricia Stephens, she is the junior minister for defence and she is entirely capable of revoking MetCo's contract if she doesn't think we can handle the vital job of City security. We have surveillance footage suggesting that the Mariner was inside the Wall, Akharee. *Inside.* He was on his way back through the Gullet when the alarms went off."

Singh looked stunned. "But that's not possible."

"And that's not even the most pressing issue," Remick went on. "If you'd bothered to look through your own blasted window in the past fifteen minutes, you'd see that we have another problem on our hands."

Singh winced, turning to look down into the Pavilion. Kara angled herself, peering over his shoulder.

The Pavilion was the heart of the Shanties, a quarter-mile expanse of flat concrete that was the closest they had to a town square. It was always busy at this time of day as weary workers were spat out of the City through the Gullet, the only tunnel leading under the Wall. But tonight the crowds were bigger than ever, a mob gathering at the base of the wide stone steps that led down from the Zoo. They surged forward, a line of riot-shielded MetCo officers holding them back.

"They're saying we allowed this to happen," Remick

spat. "That we let terrorists run loose in the Shanties. It needs to be knocked on the head before it spreads. In a few minutes I'm going to speak to them, calm things down and show the minister we're on top of it. I could use a little backup. Honestly, Singh, her being here is the last straw; if you knew the kind of pressure I'm under…"

"I'll be there, sir," Singh said. "I just need to discharge these two and I'll be right down."

Remick straightened his tie, one hand on the door. "You're a good man, Singh. Just try to keep your focus where it belongs in future."

He shut the door behind him and Singh made a rude gesture. "Focus on this," he muttered. "*Sir*."

"He's not as friendly as his picture, is he?" Joe said, peering up at Remick's portrait. "It's weird – the eyes feel like they're following me."

"There's a camera behind the left one," Singh admitted. "It's one of his favourite sayings: a family watches over each other. That's how he likes to think of us. One big MetCo family."

"Well, he does tell you off when you've been naughty," Kara pointed out.

Singh sighed. "You heard him, we're done here. Don't forget your possessions." He rifled through a small polythene bag. "One torch, one bottle, one screwdriver, one … weird plastic bear."

"I call him Growly," Joe said.

"Good for you. But what's this?" He took out a damp crumpled ball of white paper, unfolding it. A scrawl of black ink formed a crude oval filled with wavy lines. A short list of words were smudged with what might have been chocolate.

"It's just a picture," Joe said quickly. "I drew it for school."

"A picture? Of what?"

"Some…" Joe struggled. "Some spaghetti. See, it's on a plate."

"Why would you draw spaghetti?" Kara asked.

Joe looked at her intently. "I was hungry."

"And what about these words?" Singh wondered, tracing with his finger. "*Sun four, six down, news, Wellington*? What does all that mean?"

"They were already on it," Joe said. "We use old scraps at school. Haven't you heard of recycling?" He looked at Singh, unblinking. The officer folded the paper and handed it to him.

"You're a weird kid," he said. "But that's hardly a crime. OK, if you remember anything else you know where to find me. In the meantime, I'll have your boss brought from holding. But I want you to think long and hard before you get mixed up with men like him. I know you have to eat, but there's ways and there's ways, understand?"

Kara held his gaze for a moment, then she nodded. "Thank you."

Singh sighed. "Now split. I've got an angry mob to deal with."

4

The Walk
Home

They found Colpeper waiting by the security barrier in the Zoo. His left eye was black and his lip was split. "This has not been a good day," he growled as they pushed through a set of high glass doors and out into the Pavilion.

At the base of the steps the mob had tripled in size, many of the protesters still wearing their brown work overalls. They churned like a muddy sea, breaking against a wall of MetCo riot shields.

Then the shouts subsided and a murmur ran through the crowd. Kara turned to see Remick emerging from the glass facade of the Zoo, Singh at his side. Just inside stood the minister, watching darkly. Above them the Wall rose, sheer and white.

"I thought it was time I came out and said a few words." Remick spoke into a handheld microtransmitter, his voice picked up by speakers all around the Pavilion.

"It's past time!" someone shouted, and the crowd muttered their agreement.

Remick nodded. "You're right. I'm sorry. It's been quite a day."

Kara studied the man, trying to size him up. Outwardly there was nothing remarkable about him – medium height, medium build, his clothes sharp but not flashy, his hair faintly ridiculous. But the way he presented himself was powerful somehow; she couldn't imagine him ever being nervous or frightened or lost for words.

"I get why you're angry," Remick went on, his voice betraying a hint of a Shanty accent. "You all know my history with these Mariners. No one could be more determined than I am to see them driven from our waters."

Kara knew the story, everyone in the Shanties did – how as a young naval officer Remick had been captured by the Mariners and tortured half to death, how he'd escaped using his wits and risen to become head of the most powerful security corporation in the City. She didn't know how much of it was true, but everyone believed it and that was what mattered.

"Here at MetCo we work hard to keep the Shanties safe," he insisted. "With the support of our friends in government we have a mission to ensure that London remains peaceful and prosperous, inside the Wall and out. But these Mariner extremists are getting bolder all the time. Led by this thug John Cortez −" he paused for a wave of scattered booing − "they seem determined to harass us, intimidate us, undermine our way of life. We don't know why they were here today; whatever they were after we don't believe they got it. But their very presence here is an affront."

Kara could feel the crowd's anger shifting, turning away from Remick and back towards the Mariners. She saw one man spit on the concrete, a young woman balling her fists.

"Now I'm not going to tell you to go home," Remick said. "Stay if you want. Voice your frustration. But do it calmly. Peaceful protest is the right of any free society. And that's what we have here, isn't it? It's why the Mariners hate us so much. Mudfoots, they call us. Like it's an insult. I don't know about you, but I'm proud to feel solid ground under my feet. I'm proud of my MetCo family. And most of all, I'm proud to live in the greatest city on Earth."

To Kara's amazement some of the demonstrators began to clap − moments ago they'd been screaming with rage, now they were on Remick's side. He'd made them feel safe, she realised, like their concerns were being listened to. He'd given them nothing but words, but it seemed to be enough. She wondered where he'd learned to do that, and if anyone could pick it up.

As the mob dispersed they headed for Deepcut Dock, the cluster of stone jetties where the Pavilion narrowed into the neon-lit Boardwalk. A wide wooden walkway jutting just above the waterline, the Boardwalk ran right round the Wall from the Pavilion in the north to the Badlands in the south. Along it the crowds moved both ways, the majority of them heading home while others were just setting out for the night. Kara saw security guards and haulage crews, and others on less respectable errands. The food stalls were doing a roaring trade, the air filled with the greasy stink of fried fish. She felt her stomach rumble, but they had no food and no money to buy any.

Joe yawned, dead on his feet. A pair of heavily tattooed Shore Boys came barrelling towards them, machine guns slung, driftwood necklaces rattling. Kara held her course, avoiding eye contact but refusing to step aside. One of them slammed past and she took the impact, feeling a flush of pride. She hadn't given an inch, and that counted for a lot in the Shanties.

"Mariners on our doorstep!" a voice cried, a news

vendor bellowing the headlines from the doorway of his tarpaulin shack. "Are MetCo doing enough to prevent more attacks? Get all the latest from the City's most reputable sources!" A chem-generator rattled and inside Kara could see screens flickering, the broadcasts relayed from within the Wall to a crowd of eager punters. Joe tried to peer in but the vendor shooed him away. "Cough up or get lost."

Kara glowered. "We saw it already, anyway."

They reached Euston Lock and turned north, the crowds thinning as the walkways divided and divided again, tributaries branching from the river of people. The sun brushed the horizon and light slanted between the crumbling concrete towers, dappling the water with streaks of pale gold. The air was hazy with smoke from countless cook-fires and communal braziers, and Kara heard snatches of laughter, shouts of anger and the shrieks of children.

Colpeper stalked behind them muttering to himself. He hadn't said a word about what had happened, but Kara suspected it was only because he didn't want to lose his temper in public.

In front of Osborne House a young busker with tall black hair stood plucking his guitar, a rolling march for the walk home. He called himself the Pompadour, and sometimes when he played Kara got a tingling feeling down in her stomach. But tonight he was almost drowned out by Mr Shoji the soup vendor, bellowing his teatime bargains to the half-empty courtyard.

"That smells so good," Joe said, smiling sleepily. "Can we get some, Mr Colpeper?"

The big man stopped and Kara felt her stomach tighten. Colpeper's black eye gleamed in the lamplight. "After everything that happened today, you think I'm going to buy you soup?"

Joe flushed. "But … they let us go."

"No thanks to you." Colpeper's voice was hard as stone. "What were you thinking, Joe? When that ski crashed why didn't you swim the other way? When that Mariner got smashed up why did you try and help him? They questioned me for an hour. They did this to my face."

"I … I'm sorry," Joe said, his lip trembling.

"Sorry won't cut it." Colpeper poked him in the chest. "You don't seem to get how this works. I'm not your friend. I'm not your dad. I'm your boss. You work because I let you. And if I change my mind, what happens? You starve."

"Hey," Kara said, stepping between them with her heart racing, "Joe couldn't have known what was going to happen."

Colpeper's face turned crimson. "Who do you think you're talking to, girl?" The square had fallen silent; Kara could see the soup vendor watching them, and the Pompadour too. His eyes met hers and she squared her shoulders.

"I'm talking to a bully," she said, standing on her tiptoes. "You know it wasn't Joe's fault. You're just angry because MetCo made you feel small, so you're taking it out on him."

Colpeper growled, deep in his throat. She could almost see steam rising behind his eyes.

"Look, I'll help with your … project," she said, lowering her voice. "I'll do whatever you need me to do. But leave Joe alone. And give us some money for soup."

She held out her wrist, and for a moment she thought she'd pushed too far. But Colpeper sank back, shaking his head and touching his wrist to hers until she felt the chip pulse beneath her skin.

"You drive a hard bargain, Kara Jordan."

Kara frowned. "But that's a good thing, right?"

Colpeper smiled wearily. "I suppose it is. See me tomorrow and we'll talk. Until then, stay out of trouble." He lumbered away, his broad back soon lost among the shadows.

Kara spent half the money on a san-sal tablet and

a bowl of meat soup – she hoped it was cat, but rat was more likely. Then she filled her bottle, straining the water with the sleeve of her shirt. She popped in the pill and shook, watching it turn from salty brown to murky grey.

"I would have stepped in, you know."

She looked up to see the young busker standing over her, his guitar on his back. His hair was midnight black and his accent was as thick as sugar. "If he had tried to hurt you, or the boy."

Kara stood slowly. "I … I know how to handle guys like him."

The Pompadour nodded. "I believe it. I see you every day. You are a fighter."

"Th-thank you," Kara stammered. "I see you too. You play, um, well."

His eyes twinkled. "Is there something you would like to hear? A song to soothe you after a tense encounter?"

Kara laughed despite her nerves. "I like them all. I don't have any money, though."

The Pompadour swivelled his guitar and strummed a dramatic chord. "It is my gift," he said. Then he threw his head back and began to sing a lilting ballad in his native tongue, somehow desperately sad and swooningly joyful at the same time. His voice reverberated from the enclosing walls and Kara felt her knees weaken. Perhaps she was more tired than she thought.

She took the bowl from Joe, draining the last drops and returning it to the vendor. The Pompadour's response had been typical of the Shanties, she reflected – no one ever wanted to get involved, but if things got serious they'd intervene. Life here was dangerous, hectic and often bewildering. But people looked out for each other.

Kara glanced back but the singer had become distracted, pursuing two blushing women across the courtyard, batting his lashes and strumming flirtatiously. So she took Joe's hand, leading him through the shattered window and into Osborne House.

The stairwell was cluttered with people huddled like rags in the shadows. But the access corridor on Floor 13 was deserted, so Kara pulled out her screwdriver and knelt to open the ventilation grate.

Hearing a clang, she paused. A woman rounded the corner hauling a sloshing pail, smiling as she saw them. "Kara and Joe," she sang, her voice made squeaky by the wooden peg on her nose. "Got anything for me this evening, lovely children?"

"I've barely eaten all day, Mrs Davies," Kara told her. "Sorry."

"And what about you?" she asked, reaching to pat Joe on the stomach. "Anything in there for my spinach and my runner beans?"

Joe shook his head. "Maybe in the morning before school. We just had soup."

Mrs Davies eyed them with concern. "You're so thin. I worry."

Kara couldn't help thinking that if she was that concerned she could always give them the run of her rooftop garden. But it wasn't fair – Mrs Davies had thirty square feet and seven mouths to feed. And she could be generous when it suited her – last Christmas she'd given them a gull's leg and a hot bowl of beans, the best meal they'd had all year. To thank them for all they'd donated, she'd said.

She shuffled off, her bucket slopping, and Kara tugged the grate free, following Joe into the narrow shaft. Moonlight filtered through empty windows as they scrambled into the disused bathroom that had been their home for the past two years.

Kara shrugged out of her smelly overalls, selecting the least filthy T-shirt from her urinal. Then she unblocked the outflow pipe, retrieving the metal box that contained everything that was precious to either of them – a broken comwatch that had belonged to Joe's dad, a scrap of paper Kara had torn from a magazine and an ancient electronic chip reader. She pressed it to her wrist and numbers flashed on the readout, ticking upward. They were getting closer.

"Do you think that Mariner's gone to heaven?" Joe asked, sinking into the nest of rags they called a bed.

"I don't think they believe in heaven," Kara said, stashing the chip reader. "I don't either."

"Well I hope he's gone somewhere. Not just the bottom of the sea."

"What do you care? He was a terrorist."

Joe frowned. "He could've run me over but he didn't. If I hadn't been there, he'd still be alive. So it's almost like I k—"

"Don't," Kara said. "Don't even think that. He was the one who shouldn't have been there."

Joe yawned. "Can I look at the picture before I go to sleep? I don't want to dream about men on fire. I want to dream about the picture."

She handed him the magazine page and he gazed at the image printed there. It showed a white-capped mountain with a log cabin in the foreground, and a family sitting round a table heaped with pancakes. The article was about a country called Canada far across the sea. Their borders were closely guarded, but the magazine said they had an open-door policy to children, promising food and education until you came of age. But time was running out – next year Kara would be sixteen, and those doors would close forever.

Joe began to snore, clutching his plastic bear. Kara spread the picture on the rice-sack pillow by his head, then she crossed to the window, looking down into the watery streets. The Pompadour had packed up, and so had the soup stand. All was silent.

The Shanties stretched out under the dark sky, a raft of slanting lights and silhouetted towers. She wondered what must be happening down there: cops and crooks going about their business; mothers feeding their kids and knowing there wasn't enough left to feed themselves; girls her age grubbing for scraps and boys no bigger than Joe running errands for gangsters and thieves. Refugees paddling in under the cover of darkness, roping their rafts to some far-flung pier and hurrying towards the lights, swelling the population of the Shanties by five, or ten, or a hundred.

Yes, it was a rough place, but when she thought about leaving, Kara felt a pang of doubt. This was the only home she'd ever known. There was hardship and cruelty, of course there was. But there was decency too, and opportunity. You had to be tough to survive in the Shanties, and she was.

But deep down she knew that what she wanted wasn't

really important. Turning back, she could see Joe sprawled on the bed, his chest rising in fast, shallow breaths. She remembered the day she'd found him. Or had he found her? She'd been fleeing from the Sisterhood; he was halfway to being flattened by a riot squad attack line. They'd scrambled free of that churning mob and she'd known, the moment she looked into his fearful, excited eyes – she'd known he was worth more than all of it. She might not deserve any better than this place, but Joe did. He deserved a chance to make something of his life, even if it meant that one day he'd leave her behind.

Yes, Kara thought. It was time to make as much money as they could and get out, before they ran into more trouble like today, the kind Joe wouldn't come back from. Before the boy she loved was gone and a tough little stranger took his place.

5

Redeye

Kara watched Joe's back as he hurried along the bustling walkway into King's Community School, the soles of his sneakers flapping. The sun was already high, heat haze rippling from the water. She'd barely slept, haunted by visions of exploding jetskis and angry mobs, and a nagging feeling that none of this was over, that there was more to come.

She pushed away through the crowd of parents milling around the school gates, trying to ignore the contempt in their eyes as they looked at her ripped shorts and greasy hair. They were all Shanty folk, she reminded herself, no better or worse than she was. But they were workers, strivers. She bet none of them let their kids go diving for scrap.

Hunger gnawed as she hastened past a row of barbecue

barrels, charcoal smoking. An activist stood on a crate, lecturing through a megaphone. "Join the ANTIs!" he shouted, pushing steel-rimmed spectacles up his nose. "Fight against exploitation and child labour. Fight for decent wages and affordable healthcare. Join the ANTIs and fight for the Shanties!"

Kara ignored him. Those promises always sounded good, but the same groups had been saying the same stuff for years, and life in the Shanties showed no sign of improving.

Sensing movement she turned. There was a dark figure on the far side of the walkway slipping through the crowd. Keeping pace? Kara slowed and, yes, the figure slowed too.

She picked up speed, fear gnawing in her gut. She'd known that yesterday's events would have consequences, that someone would come asking questions. She was so distracted that she walked face first into a spongy wall of electric-pink stretch-cloth.

There was a shriek and Kara sprang back. A large woman stood over her, spitting on her arm and rubbing hard. "It touched me!" she cried. "The little rat touched me. I'll have to get shots."

Faces crowded in, watching Kara with horrified fascination – a tourist party from inside the Wall, judging by their clothes. And here was their escort, a MetCo corporal with red spikes in her hair. "No need to panic, madam. I'm sure she didn't mean any harm."

"She?" the woman spat. "You mean it's a girl? Good grief."

Kara felt a surge of anger, a curse forming in her mouth. But before she could speak the corporal took her arm and steered her away. "Run along, child."

"But she…" Kara spluttered. "But they're a bunch of—"

"I know," the young woman whispered. "But, trust me, the best thing you can do is leave before one of them tells me to arrest you."

Kara glared at the tourists, feeling ashamed and furious and bitterly hurt all at the same time. She wanted to yell at them, tell them she was a person too. But they'd already moved on, gazing in wonder at a heaped garbage skiff poled by a bargeman with a beard down to his knees. One of the men pretended to push his friend towards the water, provoking howls of laughter.

Kara broke into a run, suddenly desperate to put as much distance as possible between herself and those judging, superior eyes. Her rage gave her speed, pigeons scattering as she hurtled through an empty square. She could run all day if she wanted to, blazing a trail right across the Shanties. No one would be able to stop her, not the cops, not the Mariners, not those City tourists with their stupid clothes. They'd all just watch open-mouthed as she flew by, the fastest, freest thing in all the world.

Then, as suddenly as it had come, the mood left her. She staggered back, sinking on to a jutting windowsill. She drew a ragged breath and squeezed her eyes tight. The world spun around her.

After a while, Kara took her bearings. She was on a shadowed walkway between two high blocks. Water lapped at the concrete and from inside she could hear a baby crying, followed by a voice yelling at it to shut up for one second. She took a long, deep breath, clenching her fists to steady her nerves. She'd go to Colpeper and sign up to his ridiculous gun-smuggling scheme, then she'd weasel some money out of him and buy Joe a sugar donut.

She felt the presence before she saw it, just a shadow in her peripheral vision. She whipped round, goosebumps prickling her arms. A man stood a short distance away, motionless on the narrow catwalk. He was tall and slender, and dressed in a long coat of dark, leathery sealskin. His black hair fell forward over a face as pale as crab meat, but through the strands Kara could see something glowing, a flicker of red where his left eye should be.

"Don't run," he said, the accent unfamiliar. "I've chased you far enough for one day." And he smiled, his teeth gleaming. Those weren't Shanty teeth.

With a start she realised. "You're a Mariner." Even if it weren't for the clothes and the teeth, she could smell the sea all over him.

The stranger nodded. "Clever girl. They call me Redeye. I know, not very imaginative." He gestured at the crimson gleam beneath the curtain of his hair. Then he tugged back his sleeve, revealing a tattoo on his wrist – a sea-blue circle with a green oval inside it, like an upturned eye. The symbol of the Mariners. "I'm head of security on an Ark called *Neptune*. Her captain's name is John Cortez; you may have heard of him."

Kara's lip curled. "Of course. He's a pirate and a terrorist."

"So your mudfoot media claims. But one man's terrorist is another's... How does it go?" The Mariner took a step closer, raising both hands. "I mean you no harm, I promise. I just want to talk."

Kara glanced aside, measuring the distance to the water. "You want to know about the dead guy, right?"

Redeye nodded. "We know your boy Joe was the last to see him alive. I want to know what was said between them. I thought it best to come to you first, as his guardian.

There'll be profit in it, if I like what I hear."

"You stay away from Joe," Kara said, backing up. "If you so much as look at him, I'll—"

"You'll what?" the Mariner snapped, his mouth tightening. "I'm not playing games, girl. Run again and I'll hurt you. Now come here."

He lunged suddenly, grasping with long, bony fingers. But Kara was ready; she ducked and threw herself towards him shoulder first. The pale man was caught off guard, his fingers snatching at her collar. His foot swept out to trip her but Kara was already moving, crossing the platform in two bounds. She leaped over the edge into the water, his furious cry echoing in her ears.

Joe stretched his arms in the sunlight blazing through the classroom window. He was lucky today; he actually had a desk to sit behind. He didn't mind sharing with two other boys. It was better than crowding at the back with the big kids.

The subject was technology, one of his favourites. Joe was among the few in his class to have actually seen a car, though the waterlogged tubs in the sunken suburbs had little in common with the gleaming machines in Miss Ella's old clips.

The teacher stood facing them now, her hair a frizzy

red halo in the sunlight. "Who can tell me what a satellite is?" she asked, and Joe stuck his hand up. But Miss Ella nodded to a girl in the front.

"My Uncle Samson says satellites are what falls through the roof if you say too many bad swears," the girl beamed, and there was a ripple of laughter.

Miss Ella smiled. "Your uncle's partly right, a few have crash-landed in recent years. But I think the chances of one hitting you are pretty slim. You see, satellites are machines that orbit the Earth, high above our heads. Does anyone know why they might be up there?"

As one they turned to look at the ceiling where an aged fan creaked pointlessly.

"Well, back in the Tech Age, people used satellites for all sorts of things," Miss Ella continued. "Keeping track of ships and aeroplanes, sending pictures and messages right around the world. And most of them are still up there, though one by one they're all breaking down. Does anyone know why?"

A boy behind Joe stuck up his hand. "No one goes to space any more. It's too expensive."

The teacher nodded. "That's right. Oil's too scarce and chem fuel's too unstable to use in planes or rocket ships. But the truth is, most of that old tech is worthless now anyway. There's so much dust and static in the atmosphere that sending long-range signals is all but impossible. So even if someone could go up and fix the satellites, it'd be pointless."

"Will they ever?" Joe asked without raising his hand. "Will people go to space again?" The thought that he'd missed such an age of wonders made him indescribably sad.

"Who knows?" Miss Ella said. "If we can start solving our problems down here, perhaps we can start sending people back up there. One of you might be the first to go. If you study really hard."

There was laughter, but Joe didn't join in. He pictured himself strapped to the top of a great rocket blasting off into the dark. They'd seen it in a vid once and to Joe it had looked like the perfect place – no dirt, no noise, just the cold stars and the blue Earth.

He gazed at the world map pinned above Miss Ella's whiteboard. He would float over the continents, from sunken Europe and sun-baked Persia to the bustling valleys of the Himalayan Bloc. He'd soar across the Pacific until he reached America, where the flare of border wars would light up the night. Finally he'd touch down in Canada, and be welcomed with smiles and pancakes.

"Hey –" one of his deskmates broke Joe's reverie, pointing to the window – "isn't that your whatsername?"

A figure crouched on the outer ledge gesturing violently. Joe blushed as the room filled with sniggers.

"Kara?" Miss Ella asked, crossing to the window. "What on earth are you doing?"

Kara's hand shook where it clutched the frame. "I need to get Joe. Right now."

He started forward but Miss Ella held him back. "What's wrong with the front door?"

"His people might be watching," Kara hissed.

"Whose people?" the teacher asked. "Are you in trouble with MetCo again? Tell me and I'll—"

"You can't help with this," Kara insisted. "Joe, come on. Climb up."

"No," Miss Ella ordered, taking Kara's wrist. "Joe needs to learn; he needs to be in school. And so do you."

Kara yanked her hand free. "First we need to not die. So let us go or they'll hurt you too."

The teacher opened her mouth to protest, then she saw the conviction on Kara's face and sighed, kneeling to help Joe up. He peered at the water twenty feet below, tucking his T-shirt into his shorts.

"Kara, I'm not happy about this," Miss Ella said, leaning out.

Kara smiled grimly. "Neither am I," she said, and jumped.

6

Night Dive

They stayed in the water as long as they could, ducking through sunken windows and submerged rooms. In the time it took to swim home Kara had told Joe everything about her encounter with the Mariner. He was glad she'd got away, but still a bit embarrassed about being dragged out of school like that.

They came to the footbridge opposite Osborne House, crouching beneath it with their eyes on the courtyard. Like a couple of trolls in the old story, Joe thought, as Shanty folk trip-trapped overhead. Except the real monster was somewhere out there hunting for them.

"So you think this Redeye knows where we live?" He shivered, feeling the rustle of plastic and paper as he shoved his hands in his pockets. It wasn't time for that, though, not yet.

"We can't take the risk," Kara said. "We'll wait till dark, then we've got to get that scanner. After that we'll go to Colpeper; he'll know what to do."

"You trust him?" Joe asked.

Kara shook her head. "Not slightly. But if we pay him enough, he'll help us."

The day waned. Joe saw Mr Shoji setting out his stall and the Pompadour tuning his guitar, the light turning gold, then violet, and finally seeping away altogether. But there was still no sign of the black-clad Mariner.

As the moon rose they slipped out of hiding and into Osborne House. The stairwell was crowded but their little bathroom was silent and dark. Kara made straight for the pipe, plucking out the cloth and reaching inside. Her arm went deeper. Joe saw her eyes widen.

"It's not here," she said, panicked. "It's   "

"Lost something?"

They whipped round. A crimson glow pulsed in the shadows, illuminating a gaunt face darkly smiling. "I admire your determination. Waiting out there all this time." The Mariner held up Kara's scanner. "Your money's safe. And you'll have more if you do as I say."

"How did you get in?" Kara demanded. "The bolts were still on the grate."

He gestured to the tiny window. "Wasn't easy. Had to

get up to the roof and climb down. Don't worry, I didn't hurt that mad old bat. I did try her beans, though. Pretty good, once you get past the taste of urine." Suddenly he turned, sticking his hand out. "You must be Joe. Kara's told me all about you."

Joe reached out but Kara got there first, slapping Redeye's hand away. "I told you to leave him alone."

With a snarl the Mariner sprang forward, taking her by the throat. "I was trying to be friendly," he growled. "And you are being rude."

"I'll tell you everything," Joe said hurriedly. "Please don't hurt her."

Redeye shoved Kara away, straightening his coat. "Talk then. And don't lie. The red eye sees all."

He swept his hair aside and Joe let out a gasp. The Mariner's left socket was a fleshy, tortured hole, ringed with shards of metal embedded into the skin. In the depths a crimson glow pulsed, and Joe heard the grinding of tiny gears.

Was it true? he wondered fearfully. *Could the eye have special powers?* But no, the Mariner couldn't know what was in his pocket; he'd have said something by now.

"I'll t-tell you," he said, trembling. "I'll t-tell you everything. It happened out on the Spur. I'd just c-come up when—"

Kara squeezed his arm. "You were on the jetty when you first saw him, weren't you?"

She gave Joe a look so intense that he started nodding. "R-right. I was standing on the jetty and I heard the ski coming towards me…"

Redeye listened keenly as the tale unfolded, clenching his fists as Joe described the pursuing MetCo gunboat, wincing as he learned of the jetski explosion. He looked up as Joe repeated the rider's last words, frowning thoughtfully. "What do you think he meant? What was he sorry for?"

"I don't know," Joe admitted. "Before I could ask him he dragged himself into the water. He went over the side, and sank all the way down."

Redeye nodded. "That's good. I didn't like the thought of him lying in a dry grave. Unless they went down for his body?"

Joe shrugged. "It's deep there. They'd have to send divers. Maybe they did, after we'd gone."

"Well, there's only one way to find out," Redeye said, jumping to his feet and clapping his hands together. "Up, both of you. We're going for a ride."

Kara bristled. "You said if Joe talked you'd let us go."

The Mariner gave a sideways smile. "Plans change." He gestured to the vent. "Kara first, then me, then the boy. First sign of trouble and I'll kill whichever's closest. But I'll leave the other one alive so you can spend the rest of your life thinking about the choice you made."

Joe bit his lip. He felt the plastic bag in his pocket and prayed he was doing the right thing.

The night was deathly still as they emerged into the courtyard. Joe clung close to Kara, glancing up at the Mariner as he stalked alongside. He remembered a story Mr Shoji had told them once, a tale from his homeland about warriors in black who killed without a sound. What did he call them? Ninjas? Perhaps Redeye was one of those. Or maybe he was just acting that way to scare them.

"Excuse me," he said. "Will you tell us what happened to your eye?"

Kara gave a gasp, but Redeye just smiled thinly. "I could tell you what happened to the last kid who asked that question."

By the pier a boy sat on his haunches, keeping watch over a battered single-stroke jetski. Redeye touched wrists and sent the boy off, then he lifted Joe on to the seat with strong hands, climbing on behind him. He jerked a thumb and Kara clambered on the back, clinging to Redeye's coat. He tapped in a four-digit code and kicked the throttle.

They sped north through the sleeping Shanties, weaving between the dark buildings. Joe could see floodlights on the water as they passed the MetCo training grounds on Hampstead Hill, the only dry land for thirty miles outside the Wall. Redeye banked west as they approached the perimeter, where the towers gave way to open sea. Out here lived the poorest of the poor in a vast impossible puzzle of shifting rafts lashed together with rope. Often these were the same rafts they had poled from the mainland, the only homes these people had. Joe could see a group of them now huddled round a fire on a gently rocking platform singing softly. It felt like the end of the world.

Redeye gunned the throttle and the ski picked up speed. They were the only thing moving on the water tonight, save for the distant blue lights of a MetCo patrol boat. The wind made Joe's eyes sting but inside he felt a rising exhilaration, mingling with his fear to form a new feeling like nothing he'd ever known. He felt alive and free, and trapped and terrified all at the same time.

"Your friend," he asked. "The one who died. Was he a good person?"

Redeye seemed surprised. "He was his father's son. If you knew his father, you'd know that means something."

"Was his name Wellington?" Joe scanned the Mariner's face for any sign of recognition.

"His name was Elroy. Why did you think it was Wellington?"

Joe shrugged. "I thought you said it was. Never mind."

He saw a black hulk on the horizon and knew they were getting close. A tanker heaved past the tip of the Spur, running lights winking. Redeye eased down, curving into the Cut. Joe scanned the shadows, looking for anything he recognised. Then a door swung open and lamplight filtered out, followed by faint music and drunken laughter.

"There," he said. "Behind the pub. That's where he went in."

They drew alongside the shattered jetty, the timbers scorched from yesterday's impact. The water was like ink dotted with specks of warped, reflected light. Redeye lifted Joe on to the dock and Kara followed, shivering. "Show me where it happened," the Mariner said.

Joe pointed. "The ski hit that post and he landed here. You can still see the blood."

Redeye knelt, scraping the blackened wood. He put his finger in his mouth and nodded, then he got to his feet and crossed the platform. "So he went into the water here?"

Joe nodded. "Didn't float or anything. Straight down."

Redeye closed his eyes, observing a moment's silence. Then he looked at Joe. "I wonder, how hard would it be to find his body?"

Joe shook his head. "Not that hard, if you know what you're doing. Have you done much diving for… Oh."

The Mariner was smiling crookedly.

"You must be joking," Kara said. "It's dark; you can't send him down there."

Redeye pulled out Joe's torch, turning the crank. "I think of everything."

"But you're a Mariner," Kara protested. "Shouldn't you be able to do this sort of thing yourself?"

"I don't know the terrain like he does," Redeye said. "I've asked around; they say Joe is the best Beef in the business."

"But he wanted to go back to the ocean," Joe said. "Why bring him up again?"

Redeye frowned, the crimson glow lighting his face. "Because he's got something I need. Something important. Let's just say the world depends on it."

Joe looked up and a cold certainty came over him. Redeye was nothing like his friend; he wouldn't have swerved to save Joe's life. And whether or not he got what he wanted the chances were slim that they'd get out of this alive. There was only one thing for it.

"Fine, I'll go," he said, peeling off his shirt. "I'll find him."

He took a deep breath and jumped, and the filthy water swallowed him.

Kara ran to the edge, gazing into the black depths. "What did you mean just now?" she asked. "Why does the world depend on it?"

Redeye shook his head. "That's for you to find out. And believe me, you will."

Kara's eyes narrowed. "That business yesterday was just the start, wasn't it? You're planning something, you and that creep Cortez. I bet you're going to blow up a ship or kill the prime minister or something. You Mariners are all the same."

Redeye sighed. "You don't know what you're talking about. Most Mariners are just hard-working people living ordinary lives, whether on land or at sea. They couldn't care less what happens to some mangy mudfoots half a world away. But me and Cortez, we're different."

Kara raised an eyebrow. "You're saying you care about the Shanties?"

"Precisely." Redeye turned away. "We care so much we're willing to kill for it."

Kara heard a sound, just a ripple in the water. A white

blur rose from the black, ducking behind a pile of twisted timbers. "I see him!" she cried, pointing the opposite way.

Redeye hurried over. "There," Kara said as Joe slipped out of hiding behind them. "Past that skiff. He's got something."

Redeye leant out, squinting hard. "I don't see anything. Are you——"

Joe sprang forward, Kara stepped in and they both gave a shove. Redeye hit the water with a cry, limbs thrashing, his long coat tangling round his body. Kara ran for the jetski, grabbing her box and preparing to bolt. But Joe pushed her back, leaping on to the ski and reaching for the controls.

"What are you doing?" Kara yelled. "You don't know how to drive it; you need a code."

Joe tapped the keypad and the engine rattled into life. "I watched him. Come on."

Kara jumped on to the pillion seat as Redeye was climbing from the water, his coat sopping. Joe reached for the accelerator. The engine rumbled but the jetski barely moved, creeping away from the pier at walking pace. He kicked again and they picked up speed, but not enough.

"Gears!" he shouted. "Where are the gears?"

Kara looked back, seeing Redeye lurching along the

jetty into the shadow of the Last Gasp. They rattled slowly into the Cut, following the walkway. Joe stabbed frantically at the controls, to no avail. They began to drift closer, carried by the current.

Redeye re-emerged, a dark shape among deeper shadows. He ran to the edge.

"He's going to jump," Kara told Joe. "You have to do something."

Joe grabbed the handlebar, twisting in frustration. The jetski shot forward.

Kara was almost thrown back into the water but she grabbed Joe and clung on as they thundered towards the low walkway. He tried to steer clear but they were moving too fast.

"I don't know how to make it stop!" he cried. "Duck!"

Kara threw herself down as they shot beneath with inches to spare. She caught a glimpse of Redeye's startled face as they rocketed into the echoing darkness. Then she heard feet pounding on the planks overhead. "Joe, floor it! He's going to—"

Redeye sprang from the platform, spanning six feet of water in a single open-legged bound. He slammed into the moving jetski, grabbing Kara with both hands. But his grip was weak and he slid back towards the churning water, scrabbling on the wet plastic.

"Shake him off," Kara yelled and Joe banked left, weaving through a nest of pilings. Redeye was barely hanging on, water filling his eyes and his mouth. But with a superhuman effort he managed to pull himself up, both hands on the back of the ski.

Kara kicked back with all her might, but she was unsteady and her aim was poor. Redeye grabbed her ankle, shaking it, trying to tug her loose.

Joe cut round the prow of a tall tower. Kara clung to him, Redeye's hand locked round her ankle. He gave a tug and she slipped back, clutching at Joe's shirt.

The Mariner rose behind her. His hair whipped loose around his head. He shifted his balance as the jetski tipped and banked. Kara looked up into his red, gleaming eye. His hands reached for her. Then she heard Joe's soft voice in her ear. "Get down."

Kara ducked. There was a wet smack, and when she looked up Redeye was gone. The roar of the engine filled her ears as they shot beneath a low platform.

Craning her neck, Kara could see the Mariner on his back in the water, spinning slowly as they powered away. Joe let out a cry of triumph. Kara hugged him. The jetski hurtled off into the night.

7

Shore Boys

"Hang on, hang on, I'm coming." Colpeper's voice echoed up through the steel hatch and Kara heard the rattle of bolts. "D'you have any idea what time…? Oh, it's you." He raised the hatch, blinking in the pre-dawn cold.

"Let us in," Kara said. "Quick, they could be watching."

Colpeper backed down the ladder and Joe lowered the hatch behind them. The room below was dry and warm and lit with a dancing chem-lantern.

"Who's watching?" Colpeper asked. "What's going on?"

Kara shivered. "Give us a drink and I'll tell you," she said. "Something hot."

They hunkered on the edge of a battered sofa, the salt drying in their hair. From floor to ceiling, the large concrete room was heaped with salvage – engine parts and rubber tyres, barrels of screws and bolts, bags overflowing with musty clothes and even, Kara noticed, an entire shelf of books. The couch was an island in a sea of trash.

Colpeper pressed mugs of warm chicory into their hands and Kara drank, the heat flooding through her tired limbs. "So come on," he said, wrapping a mildewed blanket round his shoulders, "what's so urgent you needed to knock me up in the evil hours?"

Kara started the story and Joe finished it, Colpeper's eyes growing wider with each twist. When they reached the part where Redeye hit his head on the low beam he almost clapped. "They should turn it into an action flick," he grinned. "But this Redeye, you don't think he's dead?"

"He took a hit, but he's tough," Kara said. "And anyway, I bet there's more of them. Whatever he was looking for, he said the world depended on it."

Joe swallowed. "Kara, I…" he said, his face reddening. "I maybe should've…"

Guiltily he reached into his pocket and drew out Singh's evidence bag, unfolding it on his knee. Inside Kara recognised the drawing he'd been carrying the day before, an indecipherable tangle of lines and crosses. "Your spaghetti drawing," she said. "What does that have to do with…"

"I didn't draw it," Joe admitted, shamefaced. "That Mariner gave it to me. Elroy."

Kara gripped the sofa, her knuckles turning white. "Why didn't you say anything?"

"You weren't there," Joe said. "He was so scared. I was the last person he'd ever see. It felt … special. I didn't think it was important, but I didn't want the cops to take it so I pretended I drew it. Then when Redeye showed up I knew it meant something, but I knew for sure he shouldn't get it."

"But he was going to throttle me," Kara said incredulously.

"I nearly gave it to him then. But then he wanted to go to the Spur, and it seemed like if we went there we'd have a better chance of getting away. And we did."

Kara drew the paper out, inspecting it from every angle. It was just a jumble of lines and those few scrawled words. In one place, near what she guessed was the bottom, a cross had been marked.

Colpeper's brow furrowed. "It might be a map."

Joe's eyes lit up. "Could it lead us to buried treasure?"

"I don't know about that," Colpeper mused. "But these lines could be roads."

"I thought roads were mostly straight," Kara said. "These are all wiggly."

"What about the words?" Joe asked. "*Sun four, six down, news, Wellington?*"

"Is that an 'n'?" Colpeper squinted at the smudged lettering. "Could be 'sud four', or 'sug'. But those don't mean much either."

"Well, whatever it is," Kara said, folding the paper into her pocket, "the Mariners aren't going to stop until they've got it. You have to help us get out of the Shanties."

"What for?" Colpeper asked, surprised. "If this paper's so important you should make them pay for it. I could go with you, work out a deal. On commission, of course."

"And what makes you think they won't kill us all just for having seen it?" Kara objected. "This Redeye isn't messing around."

Colpeper shrugged. "You're the boss. Let's see how much money you got."

She handed him the scanner and Colpeper's eyebrows shot up as he checked the readout. "If I'd known about this I'd have been paying you less."

"How far can it get us?" Kara asked. "To Canada?"

He frowned. "It'll be tight, but maybe. You'll need papers, but I know where to get 'em. Why not grab some rest? I'll wake you in a few hours."

"Can't we go now?"

"It's the middle of the night," Colpeper laughed. "And these aren't the kind of people you just drop in on. I'll send a runner to make us an appointment, and by morning everything'll be sorted."

He left the room, the door swinging behind him. Joe sat slumped on the sofa, his eyes drooping. "Hey," he said sleepily. "I just thought of something. When I was telling Redeye what happened to his friend, why did you make me skip the first part?"

Kara shrugged. "I didn't know how he'd react if he found out the guy died saving some mudfoot's life."

Joe nodded, and soon his breath began to slow. Kara knew she should stay awake; what if Colpeper tried to trick them somehow? But the warmth of the room and the ticking of the clock soon hypnotised her into a deep and dreamless sleep.

By dawn they were on the move, passing over the bridge at Camden Lock and on to the broad thoroughfare that led down towards Regent's Village. This was the oldest part of the Shanties, Joe knew, the buildings purposely reclaimed to house the first waves of City workers after the barriers broke. It was the poshest part too, and Kara paused to tuck in her shirt.

"I hate these fancy places," she said. "They make me feel poor and dirty."

"You are poor and dirty," Colpeper pointed out.

"I know, but they don't have to rub my face in it, do they? They pee out the window like everyone else."

"Actually," Joe said, "Miss Ella told me some of them go indoors now."

Kara pulled a face. "That's disgusting."

Joe trotted along, marvelling at the sturdy purpose-built walkways and windows with actual glass in them. "Is this what it's like inside the Wall?" he asked Colpeper.

The big man chuckled. "This may be a better class of slum, but it's still a slum. Inside, things are … well, different."

"You've been there?" Kara asked.

Colpeper nodded. "When I was a boy. The Shanties were fairly new then; they didn't keep the City locked down like they do today. My dad was a caretaker for one of the big banks and once in a while they'd let them bring their kids in, so they could see where they'd be working when they grew up. That didn't last long. One too many Shanty rats went off on a robbing spree."

"What was it like?" Joe asked softly.

Colpeper shrugged. "Like something from a history book. Everything just like it used to be, before the world fell. The shops, the houses, the cars… It was paradise, really. The sort of place you could spend your whole life trying to get back to."

"So why didn't you? Your dad could've got you a job. You could be in there every day."

Colpeper shook his head. "Cleaning up another man's mess is no way to live."

"So you get kids to do your dirty work instead," Kara muttered.

They approached a gantry between two white-brick towers, the way barred with reinforced iron gates. A man stood guard; he wore a necklace of polished driftwood and had a starfish tattoo below his right eye. A Shore Boy, Joe realised. They were the biggest gang in the Shanties, descendants of the first Beefs who'd made a fortune plundering the seabed. Every illegal operation outside the Wall, every dodgy deal and criminal conspiracy, the Shore Boys had a hand in it.

"Mr Zuma," Colpeper said briskly. "The boss should be expecting us."

The guard looked them up and down, tugging a woollen dockers' cap over his huge bald head. Then he touched a panel on the wall and the gate ground open. "Follow. But no sudden moves."

They passed between the towers. High windows looked

down, and Joe could see armed men in every one. He felt a tightening in his gut, a sense that they were walking into a situation they couldn't possibly predict. Then they emerged from the shadows and he heard Kara gasp in surprise.

Across an expanse of courtyard a building rose three storeys from the water, its outer wall plastered with the largest picture Joe had ever seen. It was an old advertising board: a beach scene with golden sand, sparkling blue water and coloured sails tacking in the distance. The floor of the courtyard was layered with little stones, patches of sand and gnarled lumps of driftwood. Green bushes sprouted from clay pots, sculpted into recognisable shapes: a dolphin springing from a thicket of breakers; a trawler riding emerald waves; a winged woman like a ship's figurehead.

In the centre was a table, four chairs and two people. The first stood off to Joe's left – a young man holding a pair of shears, clad in nothing but a tiny pair of red shorts. Sweat glistened on his back as he snipped at one of the sculptures, a rearing creature Joe recognised from Miss Ella's books – was it called a horse? At the table a middle-aged woman lay in a reclining chair watching her companion. She wore a cotton bodysuit patterned with brightly coloured flowers, and a pair of enormous pink spectacles. At their approach she rose, flinging her arms wide.

"Colly!" she barked hoarsely. "You didn't half get fat." And she embraced Colpeper, kissing him on the cheek and leaving a bright red smear.

He struggled free. "You look well, Maura."

The woman laughed. "I look like a bag of rags, and we both know it. A working girl has to fight to keep her looks, and it's a fight I lost a long time ago." She turned to the guard. "Back to the gate, Zuma. I'll shout if I need you." Then she looked down, smiling through pearled teeth. "This must be Joe and Kara. Welcome. I'm Maura Glass. How do you like my beach?"

Kara looked around, blushing as her eyes passed over the young man in shorts. "It's … very nice," she muttered, and the woman snorted.

"Take a good look, girl. That's what he's there for. And to tend to my topiary, of course." She nudged Colpeper. "That's not a euphemism."

"No, it's a horse, isn't it?" Joe asked, and the woman burst out laughing.

"A horse," she cackled. "I love it. Sharp as a whip. You're not looking for a job, are you?"

"We're leaving town," Kara said. "That's why we're here. Colpeper said you could get us out."

The woman's smile broadened, but for some reason this only made Joe more nervous. "Right to business, I like that. I've got the papers drawn up, if you'll follow me."

She crossed to a set of glass doors and stepped through into a modest well-lit office. The walls were covered with old photographs in driftwood frames; Joe saw people and ships, streets and cars, the world as it used to be. There were sketches too, and maritime maps traced in spidery ink.

"Look around, Joe," Maura urged. "These are the last traces of a lost world. Inside the Wall they have their museums and their galleries, but that's for posh folks. Me and my Shore Boys, we're the keepers of a different history. A people's history. And all salvaged from right here under our feet."

She closed the doors and Joe felt the knot in his stomach squeeze. There was another small door at the back of the room, but it was shut too. "The forms are all here," Mrs Glass said, gesturing to her desk. "Passports, fully registered. And two one-way tickets to Canada."

Relief crossed Kara's face and she reached out. But Maura held up a hand. "Not so fast. None of this comes cheap."

Kara fumbled in her pocket, pulling out the scanner.

Maura swiped it across her wrist. "Now just enter your code."

For one urgent moment Joe wanted to tell Kara not to do it; they could take their chances. But where could they go? They were alone, and hunted. She tapped and Joe saw the numbers scroll down to zero. *So that's it*, he thought. One way or another they were in this woman's power.

Maura smiled thinly. "And the paper? Which of you has it?"

Joe felt his blood freeze. Kara turned on Colpeper. "You told her?"

The big man held up his hands. "I couldn't pass up the chance it was worth something. And you're on the next boat to Canada; you don't have to worry."

From the corner of his eye Joe had spotted something, a framed picture half hidden by the big oak desk. He squeezed Kara's hand but she wasn't paying attention to him.

"I told you I didn't want them to have it," she was saying. "I trusted you. I'm so stupid."

Maura snorted. "Can't argue with that."

"I did what's best for all of us," Colpeper insisted. "You're not the only one who benefits here."

"Kara," Joe said, tugging. "Look."

She shook him off. "What do you get?" she demanded, facing Colpeper. "We get packed off on a ship; what about you?"

"He gets his debt wiped," Maura said. "The Mariners are offering proper money for that little scrap. It's good timing too. One more week and old Colly wouldn't have had any kneecaps left."

"And what if the paper is dangerous?" Kara asked. "What if the Mariners are planning another attack? What if it means people get killed?"

Maura laughed. "All this fuss for a piece of paper and you don't even know what it means."

"I know what it means!" Joe screeched, and they turned in surprise. "If everyone can just be quiet for one second, I've figured it out."

"Joe, please," Kara said. "This isn't the time for—"

"Look," he said, pointing. "Colpeper was right. It's a map."

They all leant closer, following his trembling finger. On the wall was a framed sheet of paper printed with a tangle of coloured lines. "It's the same," Kara said, pulling Joe's paper from her pocket. The lines matched exactly, weaving round one another. "But what is it?"

Maura frowned. "It's just a map of the old underground system from back in the Tech Age. They were supposed to be gathered up and pulped when the Wall was built, but this one slipped through. It's worth a few bob but I don't see why the Mariners would be so interested in it."

Joe leant in. "This 'x'," he said. "It's here. W-Wet-Westminster."

Maura's eyes narrowed. "Parliament?"

"Where's that?" Kara asked. "What does it mean?"

"It means," a voice said from behind them, "that you're all in a lot of trouble."

8

Betrayed

Redeye's head was wrapped in bandages, his hair poking through in tufts. His good eye was so bloodshot it almost matched its mechanical twin. He stood in the doorway, backed by a pair of black-bearded henchmen; one was tall and thin as a whip, the other broad-shouldered and scowling.

"I told you," he said, lips drawing back over broken teeth. "There's no hiding from the red eye."

Maura's face tightened. "We agreed you'd come for the map after they'd gone. It's cleaner that way."

"I received new orders," Redeye said. "These children are coming with me."

Kara shook her head. "We're not going anywhere with you."

Redeye sneered. "You know, I honestly believed

you when you said you knew nothing about that map. I underestimated you, didn't I?"

"Maybe you're not as clever as you think."

"And maybe I'll gut you and hang you out the window for the seagulls – how clever is that?" Redeye held out a hand. "Give it. Now."

"Just … wait." Maura's eyes darted to the courtyard but there was no sign of her guards. "You're saying that if we turn over the map and the kids, you'll leave?"

Redeye sighed. "Well, that's where we hit a snag. Because Cortez's instructions were very clear. Bring the map. Bring the kids. And kill anyone who knows too much." He tipped his head towards the framed map on the wall. "You just had to go poking around."

His men raised their weapons – skeletal machine pistols made of fused black plastic, like no guns Joe had ever seen. One took aim at Mrs Glass, the other at Colpeper. The big man was bent double, a queasy look on his face. "Kara, I'm sorry," he hissed, his arms wrapped round himself. "I didn't mean for it to go this way."

Kara shook her head. "It's a bit late for that."

Maura had drawn herself upright, her eyes flashing as she faced Redeye. "Nobody points a gun at me in my own house," she growled. "Nobody."

Redeye smiled. "Here's to new experiences."

A shot rang out, deafening in the tiny office. Joe jumped, but to his surprise it wasn't the Mariners who had fired. Colpeper had slipped a pistol from his waistband, aiming at Redeye. But his hands were shaking and the shot went wild, striking the tall Mariner in the temple and sending him spinning off his feet.

Redeye's second henchman aimed his machine pistol, spraying the room with spiked fibreglass pellets. Joe leapt clear as Colpeper flew backwards across the desk, blood drenching his shirt. He didn't even cry out as he hit the floor, crumpling into a heap. Maura lunged at Redeye, grabbing for his gun. Joe snatched Kara's hand. "Come on!"

The door in the rear wall was unlocked and they slammed through, entering a low, half-lit corridor. Behind them Joe heard Maura cry out, followed by more gunshots. He picked a direction and they ran, past doorways offering glimpses of the rooms within – an armoury stacked with rifles and grenades, a storeroom full of stolen clothes, a barracks room where Shore Boys in green nightshirts snored on metal camp beds. He barely registered any of it; everything was so fast, so hectic, and every time he blinked he saw Colpeper's face, blank with surprise as he slid across the desk. He was a bad man, Joe knew that. He had betrayed them. But he didn't deserve to die for it.

Hearing shouts he glanced back to see Redeye ducking into the corridor, the big Mariner at his heels. Up ahead a door stood wide, and hurtling through they found themselves in a high-ceilinged warehouse that echoed to the rumble of machinery. Ragged Shanty folk huddled round plastic tables, measuring ingredients into metal bowls. A line of steel tanks were linked by industrial piping and the air was filled with a pungent alcoholic reek – the stink of home-brewed Selkie.

In the far wall a hatch stood open and they ran towards it, sunken red eyes swivelling to stare at them. Joe knew about places like this; the workers would be paid in scraps of food, but what they really craved was the strong Selkie residue they'd receive after every shift. He bit his lip. There was no time to feel bad about it now, no time for anything but running.

They were halfway across the room when more shots rang out. "Stop," Redeye barked, striding through the doorway. He fired into the air and light bulbs exploded, the workers shrieking in panic. "Give me what I want and I won't hurt you. We'll go back to our ship and leave you in peace."

"We're not stupid," Kara spat, holding up the map. "Back off or I'll rip it to shreds and eat it."

Redeye laughed. "That paper means everything. Hand it over or I'll shoot you down and pry it from your hand."

There was another round of gunfire and Joe looked up to see two Shore Boys on a high walkway aiming down at Redeye. He fired back, swinging his pistol in a reckless arc, tearing holes in the floor and the walls. The workers scattered in terror and Joe saw one of the Shore Boys waving frantically, screaming something, but it was too late.

A pellet slammed into one of the steel tanks and it exploded, spraying hot liquid and shards of metal across the warehouse. Joe felt droplets of scalding Selkie spatter across his bare arm, followed by a blast of reeking steam. Fog rolled in, shouts and shots echoing in the gloom.

They ran for the hatchway, now just a pale outline in the mist. Joe blundered into Kara and together they tumbled down a steep concrete slipway. There was a button on the wall and Joe slammed his hand on it. An iron gate rattled down, sealing them in.

He took a breath. They were in a small boathouse cut in two by a wooden jetty with a pair of black speedboats moored to it. Daylight came leaking through the open water gates. Kara snatched up a length of loose pipe, smashing the door controls to pieces. "That should hold them."

They sprinted to the nearest speedboat, hopping over the gunwale. Kara knelt beneath the dash, using her pipe to knock the housing loose. She tugged out a nest of wires, working quickly and methodically. Joe had heard of her skill as a thief, but she'd always kept that side of herself hidden from him. There was a strange expression on her face as she worked. It almost looked like happiness.

Then he heard muffled voices and the pounding of fists, and saw the hatch rising an inch, then two. Blood-stained fingers scrabbled through the gap, then it slammed down and he heard a yell.

"Come on, you piece of junk," Kara hissed. There was a spark and the speedboat's engine coughed once, twice, then died. The hatch rose another few inches, a red eye peering through, followed by the barrel of a gun.

Then the motor caught, roaring into life. Joe crouched in the passenger seat as pellets whined, tearing chunks from the fibreglass hull. He tugged the plastic bear from his pocket, clutching him in both hands as Kara gunned the throttle and they surged forward, barrelling into the sunlight.

Joe twisted, looking back over his shoulder. In the shadow of the boathouse he could see Redeye ducking beneath the hatch. He leapt into the other boat, tossing the towline free. His companion followed, the boat tipping as he squeezed into the driver's seat.

Kara slammed the stick forward and they picked up speed, turning into a narrow channel with high-rise blocks on either side. She hauled on the wheel and they banked hard, water sloshing across the bow as they careened into another wider waterway. The speed made Joe feel giddy. He looked back but could no longer see their pursuers. He could hear the rumble of their outboard, though – lower and more powerful than their own.

"That's a petrol engine," Kara said in amazement. "Who can afford a petrol engine? We won't outrun them, that's for sure."

They were moving south now, along a busy canal lined with commercial lock-ups and storage depots, wooden derricks swinging out over the water. "Where are we going?" Joe asked.

Kara shook her head. "Colpeper's dead. Who else is there?"

"Miss Ella?" Joe asked, but Kara laughed.

"Your schoolteacher against the Mariners? I don't think so."

The channel was jammed with delivery skiffs and water taxis, and Joe felt them slowing as Kara jostled for space. The Wall rose ahead, pale on the horizon.

"It's market day," Kara said. "If we can make it to the

Pavilion, we might lose them."

There was a roar behind them and Joe turned to see the black speedboat clipping the corner of a building less than fifty feet away. Redeye stood upright in the prow, his companion hunched over the wheel. They were low in the water but the engine thrummed powerfully as they ploughed through the traffic, ignoring the boatmen screaming obscenities in their wake.

"We're almost at Deepcut," Kara said. "Get ready to jump."

Joe gripped the railing. The stone piers of Deepcut Dock loomed ahead, swarming with people hauling sacks of flour and tubs of fish, bales of cloth and crates of machine parts. Kara was right; it might be enough to hide them.

Then he heard the rattle of Redeye's pistol, feeling the boat judder as pellets struck the stern. There was a whining sound and the engine began to hiss like a cornered snake. Joe saw brown liquid pumping out into the water, then with a whoosh the fuel caught fire. He jerked back.

"Kara," he coughed. "I think the engine just exploded."

She twisted the wheel, momentum carrying them forward. They slammed into the jetty, fibreglass grinding on concrete. Joe clambered from the wreck, following

Kara up a steep slipway. He shot a glance back, seeing Redeye's craft pulling in beside theirs. Then they were over the sea wall, shouldering into the mass of people, and the Mariners were lost from view.

9

Free Fire

Kara squirmed through the crowd clutching her steel pipe. Market day in the Pavilion was a riot of noise and colour; from the Wall to the harbour fence the concrete plaza was a maze of driftwood stalls and patterned canvas. She knew from childhood that they were all meant to have licences and a fixed pitch, but no one seemed inclined to enforce those rules any more – this was every trader for herself, and the result felt as much like a battleground as a bazaar.

They came to a cleared space ringed with stalls, where Shanty folk sat chatting over plates of reconstituted meatmix and greasy gumbo. Children huddled in grimy gangs, playing games of jump anchor and MetCo vs Mariners. In the centre was a Selkie circle, a ring of seats surrounding a huge steel keg, the vendor keeping his patrons' glasses topped up as they argued heatedly about the Mariner attack, MetCo's response and the Shanty Cup water-polo final next Saturday. Amid all the morning's mayhem this was a scene that, for a moment at least, made Kara feel almost normal.

"Everyone's eating except us," Joe complained. "I'm starving."

"Well, we gave all our money to that woman," Kara said. "So you'll just have to live with it."

"You could steal something," Joe suggested. "Like that boat. It was so cool; you were like—"

"No," Kara snapped. "I don't do that any more. Not unless there's no other option."

"But there's no other option *now*. Look at that baker. She's got all her buns lined up; you could just sneak past and— Hey, it's that MetCo guy!"

Kara shielded her eyes, seeing the baker handing a paper bag to a man in a blue uniform. He turned, smoothing his moustache. Joe was right. It was Lieutenant Singh.

"He seemed OK, didn't he?" Joe said. "And he hates Mariners. I bet he'd help us if we asked him."

Kara was doubtful; whoever heard of a MetCo officer going out of his way to help a Shanty rat? But Joe was already hurrying forward so she followed, watching as

Singh reached into the bag, handing a green confection to the woman beside him. Kara recognised her too – that government minister, Patricia something, looking at her algae twist with an expression of deep uncertainty.

"Mr Lieutenant!" Joe shouted, waving his arms. "It's us! We— Oh no! They're here!"

There was a rattle of gunfire, loud as thunder. Singh's head whipped round.

Kara skidded to a stop as chaos erupted, people shouting and food flying. She gripped her pipe, turning to see a dark figure moving towards them between the stalls. Redeye raised his machine pistol and fired again, a quick burst into the sky. He hadn't come alone – Kara saw the big Mariner and two newcomers, weapons drawn as they pushed through the scattering crowd.

Kara ducked behind the Selkie keg, Joe at her side. Singh had drawn his handgun, shielding the minister as he fired towards the advancing Mariners. Then he spotted Kara and sprinted over, tugging the minister with him. She crouched behind an overturned table, quivering like a plucked string. The square had cleared in seconds; they were the only ones left apart from Redeye and his men. "What on earth is going on?" Singh demanded.

"It's complicated," Kara said, peering over the keg. A kiln had spilled its contents, hot charcoal scattered across a fallen clothes stall. Redeye strode through the flames, his long coat flapping.

"We found this map," Joe said. "The Mariners want it back. We were hoping you could hide us or shoot them or something."

Kara frowned. "OK. Not that complicated."

"What map?" the minister demanded. "What are you children involved in?"

"We're not involved," Joe said. "Bad stuff just keeps happening to us."

"Come out, come out!" Redeye's voice was laced with humour and Kara felt her temper fraying, fear and resentment welling up inside her.

"Leave us alone!" she shouted from behind the keg. "We'll give you your stupid map if you'll just go away."

"Oh, it's too late for that," Redeye said. "Captain Cortez has taken a special interest in you two. One way or another, you're coming with me."

"She's not going anywhere, and neither are you."

Singh stood, raising his pistol and squeezing off a succession of shots. Redeye yelped in surprise, dropping behind a dismantled food cart. "Who's that firing?"

Singh crouched again. "This is Lieutenant Akharee Singh of the Mariner Task Force. And I am placing you under arrest."

Redeye barked laughter. "There's four of us, all armed. I think we can take you."

Singh frowned. "He's right; we're outnumbered. Reinforcements will come but we can't stay here."

"But he told us what he wanted," the minister objected. "These children and the map they're carrying. Let's just hand them over and be on our way."

"Hey," Kara bristled. "We're right here, you know."

"Joe and Kara came to me for help," Singh said. "I won't betray that. It's not an option."

"It most certainly is," the minister replied. "I came out here for a security inspection, not a gunfight. You will obey my—"

The keg shook as pellets thudded into it, punching penny-sized divots in the steel. Selkie spilled out across the concrete. "I'm waiting," Redeye called impatiently.

Kara raised her head. "Just be honest. If we give you that map, are people going to die?"

"Maybe," Redeye admitted. "But if you don't, people are also going to die. You."

"Oh, I wouldn't be so confident about that," a voice said, and Kara turned in surprise.

On the far side of the square stood a gang of bearded men, all heavily armed and armoured. The Shore Boys fanned out to reveal Maura Glass in the centre, her floral trouser suit splashed with blood.

"Wow," Joe said. "It's like everyone we know is here."

Maura took a step towards Redeye, her eyes flashing with fury. "I told you, no one pulls a gun on me in my home. Now you will pay the price for your insolence."

Redeye ducked as the Shore Boys began shooting, clouds of concrete and shards of wood exploding across the square. The Mariners fired back, using the collapsed stalls as cover.

Singh watched in bewilderment. "How is Maura Glass mixed up in this?"

Joe opened his mouth and shut it again. "OK, that bit is quite complicated."

"Attention!" Another voice boomed through a loudhailer and Kara felt her head spin. "This is MetCo. We have you surrounded. Lay down your weapons."

A platoon of riot troops came charging through the smoke firing wildly. The Shore Boys ducked for cover and Maura waved her arms. "Don't shoot at us!" she shouted. "Shoot at them!"

The cops skidded to a halt, turning. But the big Mariner rose to his feet, a gleaming silver cylinder balanced on his shoulder. There was a growing hum, electricity rippling along the length of the tube. Then there was a burst of blue flame and three stalls exploded, armoured cops flying into the air like skittles. Kara ducked as a wave of heat rolled over them.

"A hand-held energy cannon," the minister said. "I'm impressed."

"Those are my men they're murdering," Singh snarled.

Kara clutched her steel pipe. "I think we should go, while everyone's shooting each other."

"I don't want to," Joe said as pellets struck the concrete all around them. "I think we're OK here."

"I'll keep you safe," Kara promised. "But we need to get out of here."

"Oh, I'm afraid it's too late for that."

They looked up. Redeye stood over them, his machine pistol in his hand. He was bleeding from a wound in his arm and numberless grazes on his face. Behind him all was smoke and noise.

"Drop the pistol," he told Singh. "Kara, put down the pipe and come with me."

She started to rise but Singh tugged her back, placing his pistol on the ground and glaring at Redeye. "You'll never make it out alive. If Kara and Joe go with you, they'll die too."

"That's a risk I'm willing to take," Redeye told him.

"But I'm not," Singh said. "Just take this map of yours and—"

"Quiet." The minister had snatched up Singh's pistol and now she pressed it to the back of the lieutenant's neck. "You will let him take the children. No, don't turn round. Remember I can make life very difficult for you and Mr Remick, and for everyone at MetCo."

Singh frowned, and for a moment Kara thought he was going to stand firm. Then he sagged, letting go of her hand. "Kara, I'm sorry."

"It's alright," she said, climbing to her feet and hauling Joe up with her. She reached into her pocket and drew out the map, offering it to Redeye. "Take it."

He snatched it from her. The gunfire had begun to abate, withdrawing to the edges of the square. "Don't worry," Redeye said. "I'll be there when you wake up."

Kara was confused. "Wait, what?"

But he was already closing in, bright steel gleaming in his fist. She felt the needle slide into her neck, felt the world spin and slip away, then she was lost in darkness.

Part 2
On the Ocean

10

Humpback

"Kara?" The voice was plaintive and half awake. "Are we going to die?"

She rolled on to her back. Her hands and feet were bound. She tried to open her eyes but the world kept slipping. "Joe," she managed. "I won't let anything happen to you."

He sighed. "It already sort of did. You did your best, though."

Kara forced her eyes open. They were in a small room, pale light leaking through a porthole overhead. The wooden floor was rocking gently. "Are we on a boat?"

Joe sat propped against the wall, his hands tied in front of him. "We're at sea. You've been asleep for ages. More than a day."

She blinked groggily. "How did we get off the Pavilion?"

He shrugged. "It was all pretty hectic. More MetCo guys came and there was lots of shooting, then Redeye's friend Pavel blew stuff up with his energy cannon. Redeye carried you and we ran until we got to a little boat, and then that boat took us to a bigger boat, and they kept shoving me and I fell over and broke my bear." He held up the plastic figure. One of its arms had snapped off.

Kara wriggled up on to her feet, hopping to the door and trying the handle. Locked. She crossed back to the porthole, stretching on her tiptoes. The ocean was flecked with diamonds, the horizon just a blur between the grey water and the grey sky. "I've never seen the sea without buildings in it before," she breathed. "It's so ... big."

"I think we're going south," Joe said. "The sun's been going down behind us. If you see any land, it might be France. Or the next one down. Spade."

"There's nothing," Kara said. "It's empty."

A sudden sound cut the air, a hollow moan reverberating through the walls of the ship, making the hairs on her neck stand up. It came again: a weird, keening cry that seemed to resonate all around them, near and distant at the same time.

"Um, Kara," Joe whispered, "can boats be haunted?"

"Don't be ridiculous," she said uncertainly. "Whoever heard of a haunted b—"

Something slammed into the side of the boat and it tipped violently, throwing her back. She tried to keep her balance but the floor was too steep; her feet skidded as she slid helplessly towards the door. To her surprise it swung open and she caught a glimpse of Redeye's startled face as she crashed through, hitting him square in the chest.

The boat righted with a splash. Kara and Redeye landed in a tangle of limbs.

"Get off me," he barked, kicking and struggling to his feet. "Don't you try anything."

"You were the one who opened the stupid door," Kara complained, sprawling on her back.

"We weren't escaping," Joe called from inside. "The boat just rocked. Did something hit us?"

"Right," Redeye said, his good eye widening. He stepped through the door, pulling a rusty blade from his belt.

"Hey!" Kara yelled. "If you touch him I'll— Oh."

Redeye sliced through Joe's bonds, pausing to frown back at her. "You're very mistrustful."

She glared. "I get like that when someone kidnaps me."

"Where are we?" Joe asked. "Kara looked out but she couldn't see anything."

"We're in the mid Atlantic, about sixteen clicks south-west of Ilha das Flores," Redeye said. "I'm delivering you to Cortez. If he takes a liking to you, maybe you'll get out of this alive."

"I don't want some terrorist to like me," Kara snarled. "I'm going to spit in his face and tell him to jump in the sea."

Redeye sighed, pulling her to her feet and cutting her loose. "We get it – you're tough. But try to be smart too. There's no sense lashing out at people who are only trying to help you."

"How are you helping?" she asked, rubbing her wrists. "By locking us in a cupboard and dragging us off to meet the world's most wanted man?"

"By getting you out of the Shanties before…" Redeye shook his head. "Never mind. I was going to offer you something to eat, but now I'm not sure you deserve it."

"I want food," Joe said from the doorway. "I didn't say anything bad."

"No, you didn't," Redeye admitted. "But there's something I need you to see first."

A wooden staircase sloped up and Redeye climbed, leading them through a square hatch into the silver light of evening. They were on a single-masted fishing trawler, its sails furled. A brass nameplate read *Orca*, and at the wheel Kara could see the big Mariner, the one Joe had called Pavel.

"It's a boat," she said. "I've seen one bef—"

The strange groan came again, so loud that the deck vibrated beneath her feet. It was a living sound, full of emotion, not sadness or joy but something in between. But it had an almost metallic edge to it too, like a hinge creaking and a dog howling and a man moaning all at the same time.

Suddenly the ocean erupted, a pillar of water rising into the air barely fifty feet ahead of them. It was followed by a wall of blue-grey flesh so massive it blocked out the sun. Kara saw a mouth big enough to swallow the *Orca*, lined with glistening white ridges. There was a black eye set deep into the furrowed skin and for a moment she was transfixed – it was like gazing into an ancient, bottomless pool. Then the whale rolled and a barnacled fin swung towards them, slapping the surface with a consonant boom.

The wave hit them, tipping the *Orca* violently. Kara grabbed Joe as water sluiced across the deck, soaking them. "There she blows!" Redeye laughed as the great beast dived, its forked tail flicking up a shower of shimmering spray.

The whale angled away, a vast bow wave rippling behind it. Ahead Kara saw two more smooth dark backs breaking the surface, silhouetted in the haze.

"They were almost gone, you know," Redeye said, watching solemnly. "Humpbacks had been hunted to extinction in the wild but the Mariners brought them back. Just a few breeding pairs, kept safe in our sanctuaries. Eventually we were able to introduce them back to the ocean."

Joe smiled. "That's awesome."

But Kara just snorted. "What do you want, a medal?"

Redeye's mouth dropped, and for a moment he couldn't speak. Then he gestured out to sea. "I brought you up here to show you something amazing, to teach you what the Mariners are really about. And all you can do is throw it back in my face."

Kara faced him. "So you think because the Mariners saved a fish once that makes it OK to go around kidnapping people?"

"Kara," Joe whispered. "Please don't."

"Don't what?" she snapped. "What's he going to do that he hasn't done already? Shoot me?"

"We don't shoot children," Redeye said impatiently. "We're not monsters, Kara. We don't shoot anyone if we can help it."

Kara hooted. "I've seen you shoot, like, ten people. Did your hand slip?"

Redeye flushed. "I had my orders. I needed that map."

"So what about the battles?" Joe asked. "Why do you start the battles if you're so against shooting people?"

Redeye was confused. "What battles?"

"Between the Mariners and MetCo," Joe said. "Like in the films. There was one last year, *Silent Waters*. We couldn't afford it but my friend told me. George Ford, he's a famous actor, maybe the most famous, he played Mr Remick before he started MetCo, and his ship got sunk by Mariners, and he got tortured, only he wouldn't tell them anything, and he escaped back to his platoon, and there was a big battle with the Mariners and he won."

Redeye stared in disbelief. "People believe that stuff?"

"It won awards," Joe protested. "It was a true story."

"A true—" Redeye spluttered. "I can't even—" He knelt, taking Joe by the shoulders. "Here's the true story about your precious Remick. One of our Arks found him drifting. They picked him up, patched him up and sent him home. There wasn't any battle; there's never been an open engagement between the Mariners and London."

"So everything in the newsfeeds is a lie," Kara said doubtfully. "All that stuff about John Cortez being a terrorist who raids our ships."

Redeye pursed his lips. "OK, we might raid the

occasional tanker, hijack the odd shipment. But every missing boat, every warehouse fire, every freaking bar brawl, your newsfeeds say it's Mariners, it's terrorists, it's Cortez."

"So what happened in the harbour the other day?" Kara asked. "Come on, it's not like we can do anything about it now. Your friend Elroy was inside the Wall, we heard Remick say so. He must've set off that explosion to distract MetCo, but it didn't work. And you weren't with him or you'd have reacted when Joe said 'Wellington'. I think Elroy's map leads to something in the City. I think the words are clues, and he kept them vague in case he was captured. I think you're planning something big. Bigger than any tanker raid."

Redeye glared at her. "You shouldn't think so much. It'll get you in trouble."

"Hey," the big Mariner broke in, pointing towards the horizon. "They're here."

Kara shielded her eyes. There was a shadow on the water, just a speck against the setting sun. Stilling her breath she could hear the throbbing of engines, low and powerful.

"What is it?" Joe asked. "A ship?"

"Not exactly." Redeye handed him a pair of macrobinoculars. "It's home."

Joe squinted through them, twisting the focus wheel. "I see something." He drew back in surprise. "Whoa. It's really big. Is it a tanker?"

"That is the Ark *Neptune*," Redeye said proudly. "The largest vessel in the Mariner fleet. The ship in the centre we call the Hub, she's got sixteen solar turbines, twenty-three upper decks and seven lower, two thousand tons of pure haulage. But that's not the good part. Look down."

Joe angled the binoculars. "There's something on the water. The ship's pulling it along!"

"That's the Disc," Redeye said. "And it's pulling *and* pushing, and lifting and towing at the same time. The Hub is just the engine. The Disc is where it all happens."

Kara took the binoculars, her heart thumping. At first she could see nothing, just shades of grey and gold. Then something obscured her view and her mouth fell open. Joe was right. The Ark was huge.

The upright shape in the centre did resemble an ocean-going tanker, its steel sides lined with portholes and bristling with radio antennae, crane emplacements and a pair of mounted defence cannons. But extending from the tanker's upper deck she could see a slender metal spike like the mast of a sailing ship. From its tip sprouted a web of cables branching out and down towards the ocean's surface. And suspended from those wires was another larger object floating on the surface of the sea – a raft, maybe, but a huge one, many thousands of feet across.

An image flashed into her mind, a story the Sisters used to read about a bear who floated down the river in an upside-down umbrella. This was the same principle, except that the umbrella was wider than two tower blocks and there was a ship in the middle instead of a handle.

The raft was pale blue and dotted with semicircular domes, like blisters on skin. Dark shapes moved on its surface. "I see people," Kara said in disbelief. "There are people on it."

"Of course there are," Redeye said. "That's the whole point. Think of it like a village, a settlement. A town that floats."

The front of the raft – the Disc, he'd called it – was cut open in a deep V, forming an artificial harbour. If the *Neptune* kept its course, this inlet would swallow the *Orca* whole. The engines hummed louder and she felt Joe's hand wriggle down into hers, clinging on tight.

11

The Neptune

The Ark drew closer, filling the western horizon. The Disc slid over the surface of the sea, suspended on the cables branching down from overhead. A floating town, Joe marvelled. Filled with living, breathing Mariners.

He could see them clearly now, turning to look as the trawler entered the harbour. At first glance they didn't look so different from the people back home – their skin came in all the usual colours and they had the same number of arms and legs. But they wore dark, almost military-looking uniforms, and he noticed that many had pistols clipped to their waists. They ranged from kids Kara's age to weather-faced old folks, though the majority were just regular grown-ups.

The *Orca* came to a gentle stop and Redeye hit a switch, a steel gangplank rattling from the side. Joe glanced uncertainly at Kara but she just shrugged. What choice did they have?

They descended cautiously, all eyes on them. The Disc was springy, Joe's sneakers sinking almost an inch into the rubbery blue surface. The sun had set and lights were starting to blink on across the *Neptune*, pale green like flickers of phosphorescence. He heard a seagull screech and wondered how it must appear from way up there, this ring of lights surrounded by darkness. Then he realised exactly what it would look like – a blue circle with a green oval inside. The Mariner symbol, the same one he saw pinned to the uniform of every person here.

"Where's the captain?" Redeye asked, scanning the watchful faces. "Where's Cortez?"

"He's resting." The girl who stepped forward was taller than Kara, but she couldn't have been much older. She wore close-fitting black overalls and there was something in the tilt of her head and her tea-dark skin that Joe found strangely familiar. "He was out all night in one of the submersibles, and left strict instructions not to be disturbed."

Redeye looked around at the empty ocean. "He took a sub out here? At night? Why?"

The girl shrugged. "My father keeps his own counsel. You should know that by now."

"Well, he'll want to see me," Redeye said. "These two as well."

"Why?" The girl glanced sharply at Kara and Joe. "What's so special about them?"

Redeye shook his head. "Sorry, Cane, that's classified."

The girl's eyes widened. "They were there, weren't they? When my brother … when Elroy…"

That was it, Joe realised. She had the same narrow face, the same determined eyes as the young man on the jetty. He wondered how many years they'd had between them; four or five at most.

Then another thing the girl had said filtered through. *My father*. She'd been talking about John Cortez, the one the newsfeeds said was a terrorist. She was his daughter, which meant that the man who saved Joe's life had been his son. There was clearly more to all this than he'd realised.

"I can't say anything until I talk to the captain," Redeye said, starting forward. "He ordered these kids to be brought to him, and as head of security it's my duty to—"

"*Former* head of security," the girl interrupted. "You handed your duties to Mr Hillard when you left, but he's in the infirmary recovering from something he picked up at a mudfoot tavern in Pontevedra. In his absence, the

110

captain put me in charge."

"But … you're a child," Redeye protested.

Cane's face reddened. "I'm of age. I'm a sophomore cadet, and—"

"Listen," Kara cut in, stepping between them. "Can we just see Cortez and get this over with? We're tired and I've had enough."

The girl's lip curled. "Quiet, mudfoot. My father is not to be interrupted. He's in mourning for his son, the one your people killed."

"I was there," Kara told her. "But then *your* people shot at us and kidnapped us and we still don't really know why, so I think we've got a right to be annoyed. If we can't see him, can we at least lie down somewhere?"

"Somewhere with food," Joe put in.

A thought seemed to occur to Cane, a slow smile breaking over her face. "Actually, I know exactly what to do with you." She turned, calling out, "Nate? Mudfoot! Where are you, boy?"

There was a commotion in the crowd and someone shouted, "He's here! He was trying to sneak off."

The Mariners parted and a boy was shoved forward. He was older than Joe and a fair bit wider, the uniform tight across his waist. His face was half hidden behind a curtain of greasy black hair and he scowled at Cane as

111

she took his arm.

"Nate, this is your lucky day," she said. "Two of your mudfoot friends have come for a visit, and I'm putting you in charge of them."

He pulled away. "Stop saying I'm a mudfoot. I'm a Mariner; my blood's pure salt water."

Cane snorted. "Right. That's why you go green at the first sign of chop."

There was laughter and the boy blushed. "I was sick one time. Why does everyone go on about it?"

"Because it's funny," Cane said. "Anyway, take these two back to your pod and give them some of that food you've got stashed. They can stay there until my father's ready for them."

"But my pod's a one-roomer," the boy protested. "Where are we all meant to fit?"

"That's not my problem," Cane snapped. "You're not in the Academy now; this is my father's boat and he put me in charge."

"And me," Redeye put in.

"And Redeye," Cane agreed. "So if we order you to do something, you do it."

The boy looked at them, his face turning scarlet. Then he threw up his hands and stormed away, muttering. He stopped as he reached the edge of the crowd, glaring back at Joe and Kara. "Are you coming or what?"

For a moment Joe stood frozen. The faces surrounding them weren't exactly friendly, but they didn't look like bloodthirsty terrorists either, especially not that boy Nate. None of this was like he'd expected – it was somehow weirder and more normal at the same time.

"Let's go along for now," Kara whispered. "We can figure out how to escape later."

Joe nodded. "I hope there's actually food this time, though."

The Mariners parted to let them through and they followed the boy out across the Disc. Nate moved expertly over the rubbery surface, leaning back on his heels to push himself forward. Joe tried to do the same, but he kept feeling like he was about to fall flat on his face. To their right the ship rose like a steel cliff; beyond it was the moonlit sea. Looking up he could see a cold ribbon of stars spanning the whole sky. The real world seemed every bit as far away.

A forest of differently sized domes closed in around them, the same blue blisters they'd spotted from the *Orca*. Some glowed from within and Joe saw a pair of Mariners pushing inside one, a curtain sliding across the opening. This is where they live, he realised.

Nate waited beside one of the smaller domes, drawing

back the curtain as they approached. "It's only meant for one person," he said. "But I guess we'll have to manage."

He clapped his hands as he stepped inside and a light in the ceiling flickered. The dome was made from the same material as the Disc, smooth and pale blue. The floor was perfectly flat and on the wall were three zipped pouches and an electronic panel.

"Have a seat," Nate said, gesturing.

Joe looked around. "On the floor?"

The boy frowned. "Sorry. I forgot you don't know how things work."

He tapped the panel and the floor began to swell, assuming the shapes of three bulging armchairs. "We call this stuff RPV," Nate said, dropping into the nearest one. "Responsive polyvinyl. The whole Disc's made of it."

Joe sat cautiously, feeling the material firm up beneath his bottom and his back. It was strange but rather comfortable. "The Mariners invented this stuff?"

"It's been around since the Tech Age," Nate said. "But our scientists came up with new uses for it. It's waterproof and it floats, unless you tell it to sink. It can be hard as rock if you want."

"It's amazing," Joe said. "We don't have anything like this where we come from."

"I bet. Your masters keep all the good stuff for

themselves, right? Behind that Wall."

"They're not our masters," Kara retorted, staying on her feet. "London is a free city."

"That's not what they taught us in school," Nate said. "We heard the rich people have all the power and they send their MetCo goons to beat the rest of you up whenever they feel like it."

"Well, at least we don't have some terrorist ordering us about," Kara said, her colour rising. "John Cortez, high and mighty leader of the Mariners."

Nate snorted. "He's not the leader of the Mariners, President Simwe is. Cortez is just the captain of the *Neptune*."

"So why does everyone round here act like he's God or something?"

"Because they're loyal to him. They respect him."

"What about you?" Kara asked. "Don't you respect him?"

Nate's face reddened. "Of course. A posting to the *Neptune* is a great honour. But most of the crew have been with Cortez for years. He's not like the other captains; he goes his own way and they admire that. Lots of Mariners support him, on this Ark and on others."

"Well, they must be evil too, then," Kara said. "Cos he's a killer and he kidnaps kids."

"That girl said you'd have food," Joe said, trying to change the subject. "Was she lying?"

Nate got to his feet, unzipping a pouch on the wall and reaching inside. "I haven't much. We're calorie-controlled when we're at sea, for weight."

Kara laughed. "So is there a really skinny kid around here to balance you out?"

Joe kicked her ankle. "Don't be mean."

Nate ignored her, handing over a see-through packet filled with dry green flakes. Joe tore it open; the taste was intensely salty, melting on his tongue. "They're good," he said through green teeth.

Kara inspected the packet. "Seaweed. I knew it." But she took a handful anyway.

"In the morning I'll take you around the Ark," Nate offered. "Answer any questions you might have about the Mariners or the *Neptune* or—"

"Don't bother," Kara said. "We're not staying."

"I have a question," Joe said. "Why did Cane call you a mudfoot? You look like a Mariner to me."

Nate sighed. "Because I was born on land. Whereas Cane, as she never gets tired of telling everyone, was born on the ocean, during a hurricane. Hence the name."

"I thought it was because she's so sugary sweet," Kara muttered.

"So some Mariners do live on land?" Joe asked.

Nate nodded. "My family are from Frisco – it's a city in California. It's where the Mariners got started; it's kind of our capital. My Great-aunt Sedna sits on the Mariner High Council, and Cane and some of her friends think she sent me here to spy on Cortez. Well, they don't really think it, but they say it anyway to wind me up."

"Isn't California in America?" Joe asked. "My teacher told us the whole continent was just full of people shooting each other."

"Most of it is," Nate admitted. "Pretty much every state is at war with at least one other. But we stay out of that. Our border is secure and we're totally self-sustaining."

"So who cares what happens to everyone else, right?" Kara muttered.

"That's what a lot of Mariners think," Nate admitted. "They say we should put our own people first, only use our tech for the benefit of other Mariners. But then there are folks like my aunt who say we're all part of the same world, the same ecosystem, we should be trying to help everyone. Unfortunately the first lot are in charge, at least for now."

"So how did you end up out here?" Joe asked. "Did your aunt send you away?"

Nate's face fell. "I'm on Sailabout. At fifteen every

Mariner has to spend at least two years serving on a randomly assigned Ark. It was just luck I got this one."

"You sound thrilled," Kara laughed.

"So you're here on your own?" Joe asked. "No family or friends or anything?"

"Just me," Nate said through gritted teeth. "And only twenty-two and a half months to go."

There was a long silence, then Kara yawned. "Look, is there somewhere we can sleep? I just want to lie down and forget about all of this."

Nate told Joe to stand then he tapped the panel and the armchairs began to bulge and mutate, the rubbery material creaking as it reformed into two flat-topped bunks.

"I'll take the far one," Nate said, handing them a blanket. "You two can share."

Joe kicked off his shoes. "Thanks for looking after us," he said. "I know you didn't really want to."

The Mariner boy smiled for the first time. "It's OK. This must all be really weird for you."

Joe grinned. "It is. But it's kind of cool too. The Ark and the Disc and everything."

"Joe, we got stolen by Mariners," Kara said. "None of this is remotely cool." She lay down beside him, pulling the blanket up to her chin. "But don't worry," she whispered. "We'll find a way home, I promise."

Joe lay on his back, her arm across his chest. He pulled Growly from his pocket, clutching the one-armed bear. He could hear voices outside, the rumble of the ship's engines and beneath it all the sigh of the sea. Kara was right, Redeye had kidnapped them, and he'd killed Mr Colpeper. But then he remembered Elroy, who'd given his life to save Joe's. He thought about everything they'd seen, the whale and the Ark, that sharp-tongued girl and this strange, awkward boy. He thought about going back to the Shanties, to the grime and the stink. And he knew it wasn't so simple.

12

Keel Run

Joe was woken by the chatter of seabirds. The pod was bathed in blue, the sun baking on the domed roof. He could hear shouts outside and the plastic squeak of footsteps. He knew he should feel scared or helpless but somehow it was just too exciting. They were among the Mariners.

He got to his feet, bouncing on his heels. Nate had transformed his bed into a table and now he stood beside it, spooning cereal from a plastic bowl, his face lit by the glow from a rectangular object held in one hand. Writing moved on the face of the device, interspersed with pictures.

Joe came up behind him. "That's a computer, isn't it?"

Nate jerked upright, clasping the tablet to his chest. "It's mine!"

Joe held up his hands. "I know. Sorry. I didn't mean to surprise you."

Nate took a nervous breath. "What do you want?"

"Breakfast?" Joe asked. "If that's OK."

The boy waved a hand. "There's Honey-os or Wheatie Krunch. We only have sea-milk; it's made from algae proteins. Not as good as cow but better than soy."

"I had milk at school once," Joe said. "I don't know the other things. Whatever you like."

"Definitely Honey-o's," Nate said, shoving the box towards him.

Joe poured them out, watching as the young Mariner ran his fingers expertly across the glowing screen. "How does it work?"

Nate smiled apologetically. "I don't think you'd understand."

"Just because we're poor doesn't mean we're stupid." Kara sat up in bed, rubbing her eyes. "I mean, it can't be that difficult if you can operate it."

Nate frowned, then he held up the tablet. "It's mostly used for accessing information. The global superhighway fell apart a century ago, but the *Neptune* has its own databanks and the tablet links in wirelessly. With me so far?"

"No," Kara admitted.

"It means you can learn stuff," Nate said. "Say you had a project on whales. You could access biology, ecology, population numbers. It's like a library."

"We had one of those at school," Joe said proudly. "It had twenty-three books."

"Well, this is like having a million books," Nate said. "Plus there's music and shows. My favourite's *Aquaboy*. Want to watch?"

Kara shook her head, grabbing the cereal box. "We didn't come here for stupid shows. Last night you said you'd show us around, so let's get started."

"You want to learn about the Ark?" Nate asked, surprised.

"Not really," Kara said. "But if we're going to escape I need to know what the options are."

The *Neptune* was busy as they stepped from the dome, narrowly avoiding a squad of Mariners jogging in formation. The great ship rocked on the water, portholes reflecting the sunlight in random, flashing patterns. Joe listened for the engines but could hear nothing. The Ark was adrift.

From the direction of the harbour came the screech of metal and a spray of sparks. "Pavel must be patching up the *Orca*," Nate said. "I wonder why they need her seaworthy again so soon."

"I bet they're going back to London," Kara said. "They're up to something, because of that map. We should spy on them and find out."

"Spy on Redeye?" Nate asked in horror. "You're crazy."

Kara rolled her eyes. "And you're a coward. Come on, let's do your stupid tour."

He started forward, gesturing at the domes surrounding them. "The big pod near the stern is the algae farm. That's where we harvest nutrients for food. The *Neptune* is entirely self-sustaining; we could survive out here for years if we had to."

"You don't, though, right?" Kara asked worriedly.

"We'll likely make landfall in the next couple of months," Nate admitted. "There are sympathetic ports where we trade and take on supplies. But Cortez picks the away team, so you can forget that."

They weaved between the domes to the edge of the Disc; there was no boundary or railing, just waves lapping at the artificial shore. "Over there are the fishing lines," Nate said, indicating a bank of steel rods jutting over the side. "And that's the gutting room, where the catch is cleaned and boned. There are only some fish we're allowed to keep, cod and mackerel and a few others. The rest are thrown back. You know, in the Tech Age people ate so much that some species totally died out. The Mariners have been safeguarding them ever since, breeding and releasing."

"So that's what your people do all day?" Kara asked. "Get fish to have babies?"

"Conservation is one of our main objectives, yes," Nate said defensively. "But we don't just look after the oceans, we safeguard plants and insects and animals as well. Just like our symbol."

Joe frowned. "I thought it was meant to be an Ark."

"It is," Nate said, inspecting the patch on his chest. "But, look, it's the world too. The blue oceans and the green land. There's an arboretum on the Hub that's full of endangered plants, and back in Frisco we have zoos and sanctuaries filled with creatures from all around the world."

"My teacher told us lots of them have gone ek... ekstinks since the waters went up," Joe said.

"That's true," Nate agreed. "This has been the biggest extinction event since the dinosaurs."

"You have dinosaurs?" Joe gaped.

Nate laughed. "I wish."

Kara gave a deep sigh of frustration, gazing out to sea. "Oh, this is pointless. As far as I can see the only way we're going to get off this floating freakshow is if the great Cortez agrees to it. And you won't even take us to see him."

"But I can't," Nate insisted. "I'm a first-year cadet. He's the captain."

Kara sneered. "You're just scared."

"So what if I am?" Nate hissed through gritted teeth. "Some people are worth being scared of. You know, I expected my Sailabout to be tough, I expected to work hard and prove myself as a Mariner. I didn't expect to be surrounded by guys with guns, like, all the time. I didn't expect to be on a crew that goes around sinking other ships. I'm serious – a week ago we caught this whaler and Cortez fired on it. Put a hole in it and watched it go down. That's completely against council policy. I could report him just for—"

"Spoken like a true mudfoot," a voice said, and they spun round. Cane stood watching them, her hands in the pockets of her uniform. Behind her hovered a blond boy the same age, rangy and blue-eyed, with patches of yellow fluff on his chin. Nate's face drained of colour, but Cane just gestured at Kara and Joe.

"What are they doing here? I told you to hold them until my father was ready."

Nate's lip trembled. "I w-was just sh-showing them around."

Cane rolled her eyes. "Do we really have to revisit the concept of me giving orders and you following them?"

"What if they'd tried to swim away?" the boy asked. "Oh, right, they're mudfoots. They'd drown."

"We can swim," Kara retorted. "I bet Joe's a better swimmer than either of you."

The boy stepped closer. "How about I push him in and we find out?"

Kara reddened. "Try it."

Cane held up her hands. "Wait, wait, wait. Bobby, didn't you hear what she just said? She bet this little shrimp was a better swimmer than you, the five-time keel run champion. Now that is a bet I'd take."

Bobby grinned. "Keel run. Good call."

Nate shook his head. "No. Bad call. Bad, bad call." He looked pleadingly at Kara. "The keel run is dangerous, you can lose your way. A shark could come. Arks attract sharks; it's a well-known fact."

"It's a total myth," Cane said. "We've all done it. Except this one, obviously. He was too scared."

Kara faced her. "Whatever it is, Joe can do it. And if he wins you can take us to Cortez. Right away, no questions."

Cane looked uncertain, then she nodded.

"And you can give Nate a break too," Kara added.

"Enough of this mudfoot stuff, he doesn't need it."

Nate looked at her in surprise. "Th-thank you."

"And what if Bobby wins?" Cane asked. "What do you three have that we could possibly want?"

"I've got this bear," Joe offered, pulling it from his pocket. "His name's Growly."

Nate peered closer. "Hey, that's no bear; it's a space pilot. He must be from the second reboot trilogy. Look, he's got the left-side utility belt."

Cane sneered. "I don't care where it's from. You'll need to do better than some toy."

Nate sighed. "Fine. If you win, I'll do your gutting-room shifts for a week. Both of you."

"Two weeks, or no deal."

Nate hung his head. "Whatever."

"So what is this keel run, anyway?" Kara asked. "Some kind of race?"

"You could say that." Cane gestured to the ship in the centre of the Ark. "From here it looks like the Disc and the Hub are sealed up tight, doesn't it? But that wouldn't work. The Disc needs to move with the water, so there's a channel running all the way round."

"You want Joe to swim round the ship?" Kara asked. "That doesn't sound so bad."

Cane wagged her finger. "No, no. They go in the water

here. They come up there."

Kara's mouth dropped open. "You want him to swim *under* the Ark?"

The girl grinned. "It's not far, if he's as good as you say. And it's a straight line, all the way."

"But what if he runs out of air?"

"Then it's bad luck for him. Like I say, we've all done it. But if he's scared…"

Joe eyed the distance to the Hub. He'd swum further countless times, with and without tanks. But that wasn't the issue. He knew how easy it was to lose your way in the dark, how down became up, left became right, and before you knew it you were swimming in circles, gasping for breath.

"He's not scared," Kara was saying. "Joe's not scared of—"

"I can talk for myself, you know," he said, feeling a sudden rush of annoyance. "I've got a mouth."

Kara stopped. "I'm sorry. If you don't want to do it, of course you don't have to."

Joe frowned. If he backed out now these Mariners would laugh at him.

"I'll do it," he said, and jumped over the side.

He hit the surface with a splash, the cold jarring him. He trod water, looking up at their surprised faces. "So when do we start?"

Bobby laughed, peeling off his shirt and slipping into the water.

"You go on my signal," Cane called down. "We'll be right there when you come up."

Bobby leant close, clutching the edge of the Disc. "It's not as bad as it looks," he whispered. "I won't let you drown. Just watch my back."

Cane stuck two fingers into her mouth and whistled.

"Or you can watch mine," Joe said, and ducked under.

He plunged down, shoving with his feet against the underside of the Disc. The salt stung his eyes but he was used to that, and at least the sea was clean. To either side he could make out the curve of the Ark, framed by shafts of daylight filtering through the water. It was like being in a massive round hall with no walls or floor, only a perfectly flat roof. He was awestruck again at the sheer size of this place, how many people it must take to run, all of them working together. Such a thing would be impossible in the Shanties, where everyone was out for themselves.

He levelled out, cutting wide strokes with his arms. He was aware of a dim shape behind him; Bobby was gaining already, his eyes open. Joe put on a burst of speed, rising until he was just inches from the rubbery blue ceiling. The surface was crusty with algae and barnacles.

Below him all was black, and he wondered how deep it went – a mile? Two? Anything could be lurking down there. Sharks, yes, and whales too. And he'd heard fishermen's tales of worse things in the furthest fathoms, giant snakes and slimy squids that would wrap their tentacles round his body and drag him down, down in the inky cold…

He bit his lip hard. Those thoughts would do no good at all. He had to focus. He looked around, feeling a stab of fear. He thought he could see light up ahead but things were hazy; it was hard to be sure. Was he still swimming straight? His lungs were starting to burn and he kicked, the chill stiffening his limbs. He wouldn't be able to keep this up much longer.

But the light was growing. He was certain of it. And in the glow he could see Bobby a few feet to his right and several more ahead. The boy's strokes were powerful, his legs curving with long, easy kicks. He glanced back over his shoulder, shooting Joe an effortless grin.

And in that moment, Joe knew the race was lost. Bobby wasn't just older, he was fitter and far stronger. He hadn't been raised on rat meat and scrapings, he was a Mariner, born on the ocean. Joe might be the best Beef in the Shanties but that didn't mean a thing out here. He could only stare as the gap between them widened.

Then he spotted something else, a silver shape coming towards them, bouncing along the underside of the Disc like a ball rolling down a slipway. Joe recognised it immediately – an oxyacetylene tank, the kind you'd hook up to a welding torch. The cylinder hissed towards them, trailing bubbles.

Joe tried desperately to wave at Bobby, to warn him. But it was too late. The tank slammed into the boy's side, knocking the air out of him. He crumpled, eyes wide with shock. The steel cylinder twisted past him and on into the black.

Joe felt the pressure in his lungs. He could see daylight up ahead where the Disc broke against the steel-plate side of the Hub. He knew he could make it if he swam straight for it. But Bobby was already starting to drift, his limp body dragging him down. What if Joe couldn't find him again? He tried to focus, to remember where he was and what was happening, but it was all getting muddled.

He grabbed his own wrist, twisting hard. The pain shocked him and he struck out towards Bobby, kicking with all his might. He seized the boy's arm, pulling him up.

But now he was out of air. With a last effort Joe turned, distant sunlight dazzling his eyes, water boiling against the side of the ship. It was too far. He'd never make it. He was dead in the water; they both were.

Then a black shape darted across his vision, like a ghost in a dream. It curved towards him, back arched like a dolphin. *I'm hallucinating*, he thought. *My brain's switching off and it's making me see things.*

The shape had blue eyes, wide open in a dark face. It smiled at Joe, strong hands locking round his wrists. *This is no hallucination*, he thought. *It's an angel. A sea-angel, come to drag me down.*

Then, like a light, he was gone.

13

Cortez

Kara stood on the Disc's inner edge as the minutes ticked by. Ahead of her rose the central ship, and between them was a ribbon of dark water just wide enough for a boy to squeeze through. Any moment she'd see Joe's skinny brown body clambering into the light. Any moment now.

"They should be up," Nate muttered nervously. "Cane, shouldn't they be up?"

Kara saw a flicker of uncertainty in the tall girl's eyes. "If your boy's messed up," she hissed. "If he's put Bobby in danger, I'll—"

"You'll what?" Kara snapped. "This was your idea. If anything's happened, it'll be your fault." She dug her nails into her palm, trying not to think about Joe down there in the dark.

"Come on, Bobby," Cane hissed through gritted teeth.

"Don't you—"

"There!" Nate cried, pointing. "I see something!"

There was a shape in the water, a figure rising; darker than Bobby but bigger than Joe. The surface broke and Kara stepped back in surprise as a man emerged, all in a rush like a buoy cut from its moorings. He had skin the colour of driftwood and his skull was perfectly smooth, his muscles standing out like knotted rope as he heaved both boys on to the Disc.

Joe rolled on his side, coughing helplessly. Bobby slumped back, his eyes closed. The man crouched between them, breathing hard. His arms were long and with a rush of horror Kara saw that his fingers were grossly malformed, strung together with lengths of dark webbing.

She dropped beside Joe, shaking him. To her relief he opened his eyes, gasping and nodding. "I'm OK," he managed, spitting seawater.

"Bobby, wake up!" Kara turned to see Cane straddling her friend, slapping his face with the flat of her hand. She tipped his head back, blowing into his mouth.

The strange man knelt beside her. With a shiver of disgust, Kara noticed that his feet were webbed too.

"Remember what I taught you," he said. "Three times, gentle but firm."

Cane pressed down on the boy's chest, once, twice. On the third push there was a snap, and she jerked back in horror. "What was that?"

Red water leaked from Bobby's mouth as the man probed his chest cautiously. "It feels like a rib. You must have pushed too hard."

"I didn't!" Cane cried in panic. "I swear."

"That's where it hit him." Joe's voice was small. "On that side."

"What hit him?" Cane started up, a wild look in her eyes. "You murdering mudfoots, you lured him down there and—"

"It wasn't the boy's fault." The webbed man stood, holding Cane back. "Daughter, calm down."

Realisation broke over Kara like a cold wave. Of course, she should've seen it right away. She'd been expecting someone old and wicked, a wind-worn sea captain with cruel eyes. But John Cortez was the exact opposite: he was trim and agile and, she could barely bring herself to think it, sort of handsome. His features were finely arranged, his gaze intense but friendly as he turned towards Joe.

"It was a welding tank, wasn't it?" Cortez's accent was impossible to place, as though drawn from all corners of the world. "I was working with Pavel on the *Orca* and he dropped one over the side. I offered to retrieve it. I never dreamed anyone would be swimming down there."

"They were doing the keel run," Nate said, ignoring Cane's resentful glare. "I told them it was against regulations."

"I thought as much," Cortez said, then he heaved Bobby on to his shoulder. "Come on, all of you. We need to get him to the infirmary."

Kara staggered to her feet. Everything was happening so fast, her emotions ricocheting from anger to fear to relief and back again. She looked up and the sky was spinning, the ship looming like a steel blade, cutting her off from everything she'd known. Then Nate grabbed her wrist and she snapped back. "Leave me alone. I'm fine."

Joe had gone ahead, stumbling after Cane and her father, following the Disc to a hatch in the Hub's side. A gangplank spanned the channel, sided with low railings. Kara froze. She couldn't go in there; it was the centre of everything, the heart of the Ark. But Joe was already inside, so with an effort of will she followed.

She found herself in a steel hangar half as wide as the Hub itself and blazing with artificial light. Cortez marched across it to a bulkhead door in the far wall, the others behind him. Inside was a white room, the air humming with machinery.

"What happened?"

A woman in cream-coloured robes bent over Bobby as Cortez laid him down.

"An accident," the captain said. "He's got a broken rib, maybe two. But he's breathing."

"Will he be OK, Doctor Chandra?" Cane asked, reaching for Bobby's hand.

The doctor pushed past her, sliding a mask over the boy's face. "Nothing I can't handle."

A machine began to chime, a green line jumping in time with Bobby's heartbeat. The doctor forced a tube down his throat, mopping up the blood that came spilling out. Then suddenly she turned, looking at Kara and Joe.

"You're the mudfoots," she said, a statement not a question. "I'll want to take a look at you too when I'm done. I can already see you're malnourished. Look at that boy's ribs."

Joe covered his chest and blushed. "I left my T-shirt behind."

Unexpectedly the doctor smiled. "I'm sure we can find you a new one."

"You'll have to examine them later," Cortez said. "There are things they and I need to discuss. Cane, you too."

The girl flushed. "No, I have to be here in case—"

"I'm not asking," Cortez said. "The doctor will inform

us if anything changes."

"Can I c-come too?" Nate looked nervously at Kara, wringing his hands. "I was just showing them around the Ark, you see. Explaining how we d-do things. They were interested."

For a moment Kara was perplexed. Why was he so determined to join them? Then she realised – he's reluctant to leave us alone with Cortez. He's scared, and he doesn't know what's going to happen. It was oddly touching.

Cortez smiled approvingly, clapping the boy on the shoulder. "We can finish the tour together. After all, no one knows a vessel better than her captain."

Nate's face turned pale and he muttered something unintelligible.

Cortez led them back to the hangar, Cane bringing up the rear. The lights in the ceiling pulsed, making Kara's head throb. They crossed to a pair of metal doors that slid open at the push of a button. "This is called an elevator," Nate said, glancing at Cortez as though seeking his approval.

"We know," Kara said, stepping inside. "We've got one at home."

"It doesn't work, though," Joe added.

The lift began to rise, moving up through the ship.

The walls were glass, giving them a clear view over the massive hangar. "The H-Hub is one of the largest ocean-going vessels in the world," Nate stammered. "The hold is so big that the whole Disc is able to fold away inside it when we come into port, or if there's a really big storm."

"It is a remarkable thing to see," Cortez said. "Mariner ingenuity at work."

They ascended through floor after floor, Nate pointing out the gymnasium and the discotheque, the lecture hall and the laboratories. Cortez repeatedly spoke over him, describing the different projects his teams were working on, the ways they were making life better not just for the Mariners, but for everyone. Watching him, Kara got a sense of absolute self-confidence – like Remick, she could never imagine him being scared or surprised or out of his depth. He was in complete control.

They passed through the arboretum, the green so vivid it stung Kara's eyes. Flowering shrubs sprouted from banks of earth and the walls were strung with vines trailing pale white blooms. Above it was a sports hall where two teams competed to put an orange ball through a hanging net.

At last the lift stopped, the doors opening on to an expanse of windswept deck. The steel spire rose overhead, the cables branching out like the spokes of a wheel. They had reached the highest level of the Hub.

To their left was a large forward-facing cabin; inside Kara could see banks of computers and digital charts. Nate started towards it but Cortez held up a hand.

"The bridge is no place for newcomers. Or first-year cadets." He checked the comwatch on his wrist. "However, there is one more thing I would like you all to see. Step this way."

He led them across the deck, proudly indicating the long-range radio antennae and banks of meteorological sensors. Joe stared at his hands in fascination and Cortez smiled, spreading his fingers in the sunlight. The webs were almost translucent, moulded to the skin.

"I designed them myself," he said. "In partnership with one of our plastic surgeons. I'm not a young man, but I could outswim anyone on this ship."

"Do other Mariners have them?" Joe asked.

"Not yet," Cortez admitted. "But perhaps it will catch on. After all, the waters are still rising."

The wind whipped at Kara's hair, tasting of salt and chem-smoke. They reached a low guardrail and below them she saw the blue expanse of the Disc dotted with tiny figures.

Suddenly she could stay silent no longer. "Why did you bring us here?" she asked Cortez. "Why did you tell your men to kidnap us?"

He turned, his blue eyes fixing on her like search beams. In his gaze she felt exposed, vulnerable. "In part it was because of what Redeye told me," he said. "I had to meet the children who outsmarted my best lieutenant. But I had another reason. A more personal reason."

"Elroy," Joe realised. "You want to know what happened to your son."

"I do," Cortez said, nodding. "And so does Cane."

"But we already told Redeye everything," Kara said.

"It's not the same as hearing it from someone who was there. According to Redeye, Elroy's last words were that he was sorry. Why do you think he said that?"

Joe shook his head. "I don't—"

Kara reached out, squeezing his shoulder. "No," she said, facing Cortez. "If you want something from us, you have to give us something back."

Nate looked at her in alarm, and Cortez's eyes narrowed. "What do you mean?"

"We want to go home," Kara said. "We have to. We're not going to tell you anything until we're safely on our way."

Joe looked horrified. "Kara, it's his son."

"And if he cares that much, he'll let us go," Kara insisted. "We don't belong here anyway. We're not like them."

Cortez smiled almost admiringly. "Redeye told me you were tough. Now I see that he was right." He leant back against the railing. "I will consider your offer, ruthless though it is. But the truth is, we are more alike than you know, Kara. I wasn't born a Mariner either. My parents were plantation slaves; I was put to work from the day I could walk. But the Mariners saved me. They helped me see that this world isn't all hate and cruelty. It can be beautiful too."

"But Redeye said you raid ships," Kara said. "And N— Um, someone told us you sank a whaler."

Cortez glanced at Nate, whose bottom lip was quivering fearfully. "Don't be afraid, you won't get in trouble for telling the truth. Yes, my methods can be … bolder than the Mariner High Council would like. I put a hole in that stinking death-ship, and I have been known to raid the occasional vessel. But tell me, Kara, if you knew that a ship was transporting guns to a warlord who was going to use them on his own people, what would you do? If you knew a freighter's hold was full of slaves heading for some wildcat diamond mine, wouldn't you try to stop it?"

"Nate said some Mariners want to help other people," Joe put in, "but some think you should all just keep to yourselves. What side are you on?"

The Captain's eyes flashed with amusement. "Both,

and neither," he said. "I am on humanity's side, Joe. The Mariners are our last, best hope, the only ones shining a light while the world slips back into the dark. If our species is to survive we must all learn new ways to live, we must strike a new balance with nature, with the land and the oceans. Everyone on this planet will have to become Mariners."

Kara snorted. "I'd rather drown."

"That is the only other option," Cortez told her. "The great cities are all ruins now, Shanghai, New York, Cairo. I've seen them. 'Death has reared himself a throne, in a strange city lying alone… Where the good and the bad and the worst and the best, have gone to their eternal rest.' London will follow, unless something drastic happens. Unless someone steps up, and takes matters into their own—"

There was a sudden sound, an air horn giving three short blasts. Cortez's head snapped round and he smacked the railing purposefully. "Good. Right on schedule."

Below, Kara saw Mariners streaming to the edge of the Disc, pointing excitedly. Beyond them the ocean began to boil, waves of white water rolling back as a vast shape broke the surface. Sunlight gleamed on a black cylinder the size of a skyscraper with a tail fin taller than ten men.

"A submarine," Joe said in awe. "Is it yours?"

"Oh yes." Cortez nodded. "She's most certainly mine. The *Kraken* is the most advanced vessel in the Mariner fleet. So new the mudfoots don't even know she exists. Yet."

A conning tower jutted from the submarine's crown, half as high as the Hub. Diving planes branched from the sides like wings, and the entire craft bristled with rocket launchers, barrage blasters and energy cannons. On the bowsprit a twisted face was painted, fifty feet high with mad eyes and a mouth crammed with pointed teeth.

Kara suppressed a shudder. "Why is it … she … here?"

"For a party," Cortez smiled. "No, I'm serious. If you've never been to a Mariner party, you're in for a treat. I'm talking music, food, drinks, lots of drinks. Tonight we'll celebrate, because soon…" He broke off, a smile playing on his lips.

"Soon?" Kara prompted.

"Soon there'll be a storm coming."

14

The Party

Clouds were gathering in a sky streaked with crimson as the three of them weaved between the domes towards the *Neptune*'s harbour. The sea was calm, the Ark lying so still that Kara could almost fool herself into thinking they were back on land.

Nate had found them some Mariner clothes – light brown robes that looked better on Joe than they did on her. He'd also introduced them to something called a shower, a more complicated version of the bucket on a rope that Kara remembered from the Sisterhood. Joe had laughed out loud when she'd emerged from the stall, her face scrubbed clean and her hair free of knots. Nate had gone red and looked at his feet. "You look ... nice," he'd muttered.

They could hear the party before they saw it, a rolling

melody drifting on the evening air. Mariner music wasn't like the stuff at home, Kara had discovered. In the Shanties they liked punishing beats and angry rhymes about the hurts you'd suffered and the wrongs you'd avenged. It made you feel tough, but it could get a bit much. Mariner music was wider somehow, grand and majestic. She could feel it getting inside her, squeezing her heart without her wanting it to.

The clatter of an outboard engine rose above the music and she saw a dinghy curving into the harbour. It was crammed with men from the *Kraken*, all of them shaven-headed and muscular, pistols rattling as they clambered on to the Disc. They laughed and jostled, bellowing a crude chant about the differences between Mariner girls and mudfoots.

"What are they even doing here?" Nate wondered. "Mariner law dictates that military vessels stay close to home except in extreme circumstances. But they're thousands of miles from Frisco."

"I bet it's part of Cortez's plan," Kara said. "Something to do with this storm of his."

They moved through the party, eyes following them, conversations stopping dead as they approached. Kara's nose twitched, smelling seaweed and spice and a charcoal fish so familiar it made her ache for home. Serving tables stood along the waterfront and Nate hurried off to find plates.

"I haven't forgotten about you," a voice said, and they turned. Doctor Chandra stood with two other Mariners, a cup of wine in her hand. "At the very least you need shots. I don't want you spreading your Shanty diseases on my boat."

Kara felt her face go red but the doctor just laughed. "I'm teasing," she said, gesturing to the people beside her. "Here, meet Lupita Dwyer, the catch supervisor. We call her Queen of the Lines. And this is Lars Olson; he teaches the cadets. You'll get to know him if you decide to stay."

"We're not," Kara said quickly. She couldn't forget what Nate had told them – everyone on the *Neptune* was loyal to Cortez. The doctor might seem nice but it was probably just an act.

"This boy's been on board a day and he's already saved a life," the doctor told her companions as Joe shook their hands politely. "Young Bobby would've drowned if Joe hadn't been there."

"Is he OK?" Joe asked.

"All patched up," the doctor smiled, pointing. A short distance away Bobby sat upright in a wheeled chair, surrounded by young Mariners. "I ordered him to stay in bed but he flat-out refused to miss the party. In fact he's been asking after you. Go talk to him."

Joe bounded away eagerly and Kara hurried after him. "Joe, I really don't know if—"

But it was too late. Bobby's eyes shone as he saw them approaching, his fellow Mariners spreading out to make room. "Guys, this is Joe," he said proudly. "He saved my life."

Joe blushed violently. "Cortez did, not me. I would've died too if he hadn't come."

"Exactly," Bobby said. "You took a big risk coming back for me."

Cane strode towards them and Kara braced, balling her fists. But the girl just pushed past her, grabbing Joe and spinning him round. "Our hero!" she cried as he laughed breathlessly, a high happy sound that Kara hadn't heard in as long as she could remember.

"I'm sorry I got the wrong idea before," Cane said. "Bobby told me what really happened."

"It's OK," Joe said. "I probably would've thought the same."

One of the cadets pressed a glass of juice into his hand; another handed him a plate piled with cake. He beamed at Kara, his mouth ringed with pink icing. "Have some!"

Instead she took his arm, drawing him gently to the

edge of the circle, keeping the smile fixed on her face. "You've got to be careful," she whispered. "These people aren't our friends, remember? I don't think we should trust them."

Joe wiped his mouth. "They're just saying thanks for what I did. They're just being nice."

"But they're Mariners," Kara insisted. "They're terrorists and pirates. And they almost got you killed today."

"That was an accident," Joe said. "And I don't think they're all terrorists. Bobby's cool, and so's Nate. And I get that you don't like Cane, but I think she's just tough, and when you get to know her she'd be OK too. Like you, sort of."

Kara bristled. "I'm nothing like her. I'm nothing like any of them. We need to stick to the plan and get back to the Shanties."

"But it's dangerous there," Joe protested. "It's smelly and we're always hungry. Here there's food and it's clean and—"

"This isn't a discussion," Kara cut him off. "I've made up my mind."

Joe's face turned red. "And what if I haven't made up mine? What if I won't go? Are you going to kidnap me, like Redeye?"

"If I have to," Kara said, ignoring the insult. "I know what's best, Joe. Trust me."

He pulled away. "Why don't you trust me for a change? I think it's good here. I think you're worrying about nothing. I won't go back, Kara. I *refuse*."

And he pushed through the crowd towards Cane and Bobby, their warm smiles welcoming him in. Kara felt her frustration rising; she wanted to storm over there and drag him away, tell them to leave him alone. He was hers, not theirs.

But that would only drive him further from her. So she turned, shoving through the party, skirting a noisy group of *Kraken* crewmen. She found a quiet spot near the edge of the Disc and sank down, nothing ahead but dark water and the circling searchlight atop the submarine's tower. She heard the creak of the *Orca*'s mast, the very vessel that had delivered them into this trap. She hung her head and cursed.

"So that's where you've been hiding." Cortez's voice echoed out of the dark and Kara turned sharply.

"Just making some final checks," a familiar voice answered and she crouched lower, ducking behind a stack of crates. "We sail at first light."

Boots descended the *Orca*'s gangplank, a red glow pulsing in the dark.

"It feels wrong, doesn't it?" Cortez said. "Sending you off without Elroy. You were practically brothers, inseparable since…"

"Since he found me in the desert," Redeye agreed. "But remember, he'll be avenged a thousand times over. They all will."

"Blood for blood," Cortez muttered, and his voice was so cold it made Kara shudder. "Now, I know you wanted more time, but after that mess in the Shanties we don't have a choice. Our friend urges us to strike now, before the situation changes."

"And you trust him?" Redeye asked.

Cortez laughed. "Oh, I'd never be foolish enough to do that. He's an animal really, a greed-driven psychopath with no more morals than a sand shark."

"So why…"

"Because he needs us to fulfil his ambitions, and we need him to fulfil ours. And as long as both those things are true he'll act in his own self interest." Cortez sighed. "You know, I keep thinking of Kara and Joe. They have no idea how crucial they've been. Without them Elroy's efforts would've been meaningless. The map would be lost and you'd never have found that back door."

"You need to watch them," Redeye warned. "They could still make trouble."

"The girl, perhaps," Cortez admitted. "She's crafty, that one. Though if she thinks I'm going to send her home, she's very much mistaken. I won't have her spreading panic in the Shanties before we even arrive. But the boy is different. He'll make a good Mariner someday. Looking at Joe I remember why we're doing all this. It's a new world we're making, and children like him are the ones who'll have to live in it."

Kara huddled behind the crates, trying to hang on to everything she was hearing. Words and phrases flashed through her mind: "*blood for blood*", "*our friend*", "*the back door.*" For days she'd been creeping closer to some kind of answer, some kind of truth. Now it was starting to fit together. An attack on London by submarine, that had to be the heart of it. Redeye was going to follow Elroy's map to something called the back door. A way under the Wall? Yes, it must be. He would pass through, and keep the door open until Cortez and the *Kraken* arrived.

So what about the Shanties? Cortez meant to go there; whatever he was planning they were part of it too. But what could she do, stuck out here?

Timbers groaned and suddenly it came to her. The *Orca* sailed at dawn, and she and Joe had to be on it. How hard could it be to sneak on board and hide, somewhere Redeye wouldn't find them until it was too late? Yes, he might try to throw them overboard, but they could worry about that when it happened. All she had to do was convince Joe that this was the right thing to—

"Kara?"

She whipped round as Joe's voice echoed from the shadows, back towards the party. "Where are you? We've got fish and bread and these fried squid things; they're really tasty."

She covered her head, praying for him to go away. Cortez and Redeye had fallen silent; she could feel them listening.

"Are you sure she came this way?" Nate was so near that Kara could see his silhouette against the Hub's running lights. "I mean, why did she run off in the first place?"

"She was annoyed with me," Joe admitted. "It doesn't matter why. I just— Hey, there you are!" He strode up, stopping as he saw her crouched behind the crates. "What are you doing down there?"

"That's precisely what I'd like to know," Cortez said, and reached down.

Kara ducked away, scrambling to her feet. Redeye stepped in to cut her off. "You see?" he said. "Trouble."

"How long have you been there?" Cortez demanded. "What did you hear?"

For an instant Kara considered denying it, but she

knew they'd never believe her. So she stuck out her chin, facing him defiantly. "I heard everything," she said. "I heard about the back door, and about the friend. I know you're going to attack the Shanties, and I know I'm going to stop you."

Cortez frowned. "Whatever you think you heard, you're overreacting. No harm will come to anyone in the Shanties. You have my word."

"I don't believe your word," Kara spat. "You're a terrorist and a murderer."

Dimly she was aware of other figures in the dark, Mariners coming to see what the fuss was. She looked up at Cortez.

"Do you want to know what really happened to your son?" she asked. "I'll tell you if you want, but you might not like it."

The captain eyed her warily. "Go on."

"Well, it happened out on the Spur," Kara began. "We were there with Colpeper, the man Redeye killed. Joe came up from the water just as your son was escaping from MetCo, trying to get away into the Shanties. He would've made it, only Joe was in the way." She gritted her teeth, and swallowed hard. "So your son had a choice, you see. Keep going, kill Joe and escape. Or turn aside and sacrifice his own life for Joe's."

Cortez made a noise in his throat, a strangled gasp of disbelief. He took a step back, shaking his head. "No," he said. "It's not possible, Elroy wouldn't risk everything we'd worked towards for the sake of some mudfoot brat."

"But he did," Kara said. "He saved Joe's life, and he died for it."

"You're lying." Cane stepped forward, pure hatred in her eyes. "Joe, tell me she's lying."

Joe whimpered, looking up at her. "It's true. I'm sorry I didn't tell you, I just—"

"Don't bother," Kara said. "I told you, Joe. They're not good people. They wish you were dead. They wish you'd died and he was still here. Their precious Elroy."

"Don't you say his name!" Cortez roared. He reached out, his hand locking round Kara's wrist, the thin webs clammy against her skin. She pulled away in disgust but he was too strong, twisting her arm painfully. She swung with her free hand, lashing blindly, feeling the nails digging in.

There was a howl of pain and Cortez staggered back, clutching his face. Blood leaked between his fingers. He pulled his hand away. Four ragged scratches stood out on his cheek.

"You little savage," he sneered. "You vicious mudfoot."

"Please stop," Joe whined. "Please don't be angry with us."

"Hush," Kara said. "It's too late."

"Oh, it's much too late." Cortez said. "You can't stop what's coming. And you'll never see your precious Shanties again." He gestured to Cane. "Take this ... creature to the cages. The boy can go in the brig."

Cane advanced, flanked by Redeye and Pavel. Kara backed away but they surrounded her, Cane yanking her arm up behind her back. Joe stared, his eyes wide and uncomprehending.

"Don't be frightened," Kara told him. "It'll be OK. Just do whatever they say."

Cane shoved her forward, driving Kara through the midst of the party and out between the domes. Drunk Mariners turned to watch but no one said a word; she could see it in their eyes – the mudfoot must have deserved it.

They came to the edge of the Disc and all she could see was the empty ocean. *Is this a trick?* she thought suddenly. *Is Cane going to push me in and watch me drown?* Then she saw three shapes to her left, low in the water. The cages were two feet square and perhaps five deep, their steel frames half submerged.

Cortez strode to the nearest one, wrenching the hatch

open. Kara tried to struggle, twisting and bucking as she was forced to the edge, one shoe flying free. She could feel Cane's hot breath on her neck, heard a grunt as she slammed her head back into the girl's face with a satisfying smack. Then she was through the hatch and falling, hitting the water, kicking desperately. Kara grabbed the bars, trying to pull herself up, but the steel trap clanged shut.

They strode away and she was left alone, up to her neck in dark water.

15

Two Cages

"You need to get her out," Joe insisted. "You need to find her and get her out."

Nate looked at him through the bars of the white-walled cell as rain drummed on the windows. "I know where she is; she's in the cages. But if I went near her, they'd stop me. They might even shoot me."

Joe tried to stand but he was chained to the metal cot. "There must be someone who'll help. That doctor, or … someone."

"I told you, everyone on the Ark is loyal to Cortez," Nate said. "They might not know everything he's up to but they're still his people."

Joe sank back, moaning in frustration. The *Neptune*'s brig was small, but he knew it was luxury compared to the place they were keeping Kara. Nate had told him about the cages, how they were as much of a form of torture as a method of imprisonment. Why hadn't he listened to her? Cortez really was planning something; she'd been right all along.

"Did you find anything on your computer?" he asked, forcing himself to stay calm.

Nate took the tablet from his pocket, shaking his head. "You can't just look up Cortez's Secret Plan unfortunately. But I tried the words on Elroy's map. *Sun four* and *six down* are too random. I didn't get any hits at all. *News* is useless because you just get the latest headlines. The only one that went anywhere was *Wellington*, which could either be a kind of boot, an old duke or this guy here, who it says is the youngest of the Wombles. I suppose they could be some kind of terrorist group."

Joe peered at the bizarre image on the screen. "Is that thing real?"

Nate shrugged. "It says he's an inventor; maybe he's created a new weapon. I sort of doubt it, though."

"So that's it," Joe said bitterly. "We just leave Kara in there."

Nate hung his head. "Look, I know you think I should steal a gun and go bust her out or something, but I'm not like you, Joe. I didn't grow up on the streets; I went to school and played VR games and watched *Aquaboy*.

I'm not brave."

"Neither am I," Joe insisted. "Kara's always looked after me. That's why I have to help her now. It's my turn."

The door slammed open and a uniformed Mariner entered, pushing past Nate. He reached up to a panel on the wall, tapping in a six-digit code. The cell swung open and he stepped in, placing a tray of food beside the bed. "Breakfast is served."

"I have to see the Captain," Joe said, straining against his chains. "It's really important."

"Simmer down, mudfoot," the guard said, one hand dropping to the stun-stick attached to his belt. "He'll see you when he's ready; until then you're my problem, not his."

Joe looked up at him. "Is Kara okay? Are you taking food to her, too?"

The Mariner laughed derisively. "Dream on, shrimp. No one attacks the captain and gets away with it. Mark my words, she'll never leave that cage alive."

Kara shivered uncontrollably, her clothes matted to her wrinkled skin. The rain had started before dawn, lashing in dark torrents. The sunrise was barely a glimmer behind the clouds, too distant to warm her. She heard the *Orca* depart, the clatter of pistons fading, rattling out to sea and taking the last of her hopes with it.

She knew Cortez would never let her out, not after what she'd done. And she knew what happened to people who stayed too long in water; cases of trench foot were common in the Shanties. Her skin would pucker and rot; she'd start to decompose before she was even dead.

But at least Joe was safe. She wondered if he'd be allowed to come to her, to speak to her through the bars, tell her how sorry he was. That desperate look back on the harbour might be the last she'd ever see of him. How long would he miss her? Not too long. He was young; he'd learn to live with it.

She slipped into a hazy not-quite-sleep, dreaming she was back on the Spur, dipping her feet as she waited for Joe to surface. She looked towards the distant Wall and saw figures crawling up, spreadeagled on the concrete like pond skaters on a pool. The Mariners meant to murder everyone inside, and there was nothing she could do to stop them.

The tide began to rise, filthy water climbing the pilings towards her. The buildings disappeared floor by floor, even the Wall would soon be submerged. It rose up her arms, over her shoulders, and then she was spitting, trying to keep her head up as the Stain came to drown her.

She woke spluttering, the water up to her mouth. The

cage heaved on the choppy sea, the wind howling. Up and down she went, until she felt the bile rising in her throat and couldn't hold it in. Her vomit splashed into the water, washing back in slimy ripples. She gripped the bars of the cage and hung there, breathing hard. Every muscle ached and there was a mist behind her eyes so thick she could barely see. She tilted her face to the sky, letting the rain run down her throat.

As night fell the rain abated, the clouds dissolved and the moon broke through. Kara heard the guards change shifts, footsteps squeaking off towards the Hub. It was no use trying to stop herself shivering, but she was alive and awake. Slowly her head began to clear, the fog and nightmares of the day breaking like the clouds. But at the same time, she knew she couldn't take another night in here. She would lose herself, and this time there'd be no coming back.

She looked down. If the sky was black the sea was even blacker, a darkness so absolute it seemed to shrivel something inside her. With an effort of will she tore her eyes away. She had to be strong, keep her head up, keep—

"Hey," a voice said suddenly, clear and crisp in the darkness. "What are you…?" There was a flash and a thud, and the cage shook. Kara looked up.

A man lay on the steel roof, staring blankly. Blood

dripped from the tip of his nose and spiralled in the water. Then he was dragged aside and another face peered through, brown eyes shining with exhilaration and terror. "Hang on," Nate whispered. "We're getting you out."

He brandished a pair of bolt cutters, biting through the padlock. The hatch swung open and he reached in, hands shaking. Kara scrambled free, falling to her knees on the edge of the Disc. For a moment the world drifted away.

Then a soft head buried itself in the hollow of her neck, hands clinging to her wet skin. "I'm so sorry," Joe whimpered. "I should've listened to you."

She found the strength to reach up and stroke his back. "Hush. It'll take a lot more than this to break us up, right?"

Over his shoulder she could see the unconscious Mariner sprawled on his back. "Is he...?"

"Just out cold," Nate said, holding up a stun-stick. "But we should split before someone comes."

Kara sighed. "Redeye took the *Orca*. We're stuck here."

Nate put an arm round her waist, lifting her to her feet. "Trust me. I know what I'm doing."

The Ark spun and for a moment Kara thought she was going to fall. But Nate held her tight as they staggered towards the Hub, weaving between the sleeping domes.

"I'm sorry we were so long," he said. "I took a bit of convincing."

"Cortez was going to let you die in there," Joe explained. "But then Nate stole the guard's stunner and I memorised the code for the cell, just like I did with the jetski, remember? And we escaped."

They reached the access bridge, the hatch in the side of the Hub sliding open. They crossed the hangar and stepped into the elevator. Kara saw her face reflected in the glass walls, repeated to infinity. Her hair was filthy, her eyes hollow, her lip split. She looked like herself again.

Nate hit a button and to her surprise the lift began to descend. For a moment all was silent, just the humming of cogs as they dropped into the belly of the ship. Then the doors slid wide and a blast of hot air rolled in. The mirrors clouded, blurring her reflection.

Nate stepped out cautiously. They were in the base of a massive chamber, steel walls stretching up and out of sight. Machines rose from the mist, fed by rubberised cables snaking out of the gloom. The air was thick with moisture and greasy electricity.

"We're lucky the Ark's powered down," he said. "When the turbine's running you can't come near the engine room without ear defenders. It's impressive, though. It's a shame you missed it."

"We'll live," Kara told him.

They moved in single file along a grated walkway between two giant machine hulks. A blue flash lit the hangar, the hairs on Kara's arms prickling. Overhead was the propeller shaft, a horizontal steel cylinder thicker than her torso and glistening with droplets. It emerged from the largest of the turbines, disappearing into the stern-side wall. They ducked beneath it, through a narrow doorway into a second, smaller chamber.

To the left and right were circular hatches, each as high as a man. Nate crossed to the nearest one, tapping a panel on the wall. A light switched from red to green and the hatch swung open. Through it Kara could see a horizontal access tube leading to an enclosed area with two rows of seats.

"That looks like a car," Joe said, confused. "Why would you need a car down here?"

"It's a submersible. There are two of them, see?" Nate indicated the hatch on the far side. "They're called *Marlin* and *Dory*. Don't ask me why." He slipped his pack off his shoulders, tossing it into the tube. "I managed to pinch some fresh water and snacks from the refectory; should keep us going for a couple of days."

Kara whistled. "You really thought of everything, didn't you? Now let's get out of here before—"

"Before someone catches you?" a voice said, and they spun round.

Cane stepped through the doorway, a pistol in one hand and a radio transmitter in the other. Her eyes had a gloating gleam. "I've called my father. He's on his way, so don't try anything."

"H-how did you find us?" Nate stammered. "I was really careful!"

Cane laughed. "With Redeye off the Ark I'm security chief again. I programmed an alert if certain sensors were triggered, including the one on that door. I honestly didn't think you'd have the guts to try it."

"Cortez was going to let Kara die," Joe protested.

"Well, maybe she deserves it," Cane spat. "She won't be the last before all this is over. My father's going to save the world; if a few mudfoots have to die, it'll be worth it."

"Have you ever actually seen anyone die?" Kara asked. "It's not like you think."

"Don't talk to me like I'm a child!" Cane said, gesturing with the gun. "I'm John Cortez's daughter."

"I bet his hands don't shake like that when he threatens someone," Kara sneered. Then she jerked her head up. "Hey, what's that?"

It was a clumsy diversion, but it worked. Cane only glanced back momentarily but it was all Kara needed –

she threw herself at the girl, ducking and slamming into Cane's side before she could lower the pistol. The gun roared, a pellet striking the wall in a flash of sparks. Nate grabbed Joe, pulling him back into the access tube.

Kara yanked Cane towards her, driving her knee into the girl's stomach. Cane staggered back, then she pulled herself up, glaring. For a moment Kara saw the family resemblance – there was such rage in her eyes, such boiling hatred.

"Mudfoot scum," she snarled. Then she charged, fists swinging. Kara ducked and the first lunge swept overhead. But the next made contact, the gun in Cane's hand adding weight to the blow. Kara hit the wall, the breath knocked from her. Cane swung her pistol but Kara recovered quickly; she chopped down and the weapon clattered to the floor. Reaching up, she grabbed Cane by the throat.

"Kara, come on," Nate called from the hatchway. "Drop her and let's go."

But Kara couldn't do it; she kept squeezing as hard as she could. "Your father's a villain," she hissed. "Whatever he's planning, it needs to stop."

"No." Cane clawed desperately, her face turning crimson. "He's … he's…"

"Kara, put her down!"

Cortez strode through the narrow doorway, his eyes blazing. Kara saw others at his back, a pair of burly Mariners with rifles drawn. She opened her hand and Cane dropped, wheezing.

"Daughter, to me," Cortez said, taking Cane's hand as she stumbled towards him. He raised a slender pistol, taking aim at Kara. "I hope everyone in the Shanties isn't as troublesome as you."

"Most of us are worse," Kara said, her back pressed to the wall. There was nowhere to run even if she'd wanted to; the hatch was too far away and so was the rear door. Cortez cocked his pistol.

Then with a strangled screech Nate came leaping from the hatchway, a red cylinder clutched in his hands. He thumbed a switch and white foam gushed out, drenching Cortez and his henchmen. "Run!" he shouted and Kara sprinted for the hatch, tumbling inside.

Cortez fired blindly, pellets ricocheting off the housing. He cried out in fury as Joe heaved the hatch shut and Nate spun the wheel, sealing them inside. Projectiles thudded into the steel.

"Um, wow," Kara said. "Thanks."

Nate dropped the fire extinguisher with a clang, just missing his own foot. His eyes were wide, his hands trembling. "I really don't know what came over me."

He retreated towards the submersible, pushing Joe ahead of him. "Get in the back. Kara, take the navigator's chair." He slid into the pilot's seat, facing a huge control panel crowded with computer interfaces and pressure gauges. "Wow. That is a lot of buttons."

"Can you drive it?" Kara asked, belting herself in beside him.

"I had a Stingray 2000 back in Frisco," Nate said. "But that was just a learner. This one's a bit more complicated."

He flicked a switch and a panel in the side slid shut with a hiss of compressed air. "Good start," he said, taking hold of the twin-handled steering bar. "Now if I just push this…"

Motors whined but the sub didn't move. The portholes were dark and the padded walls seemed to close in. Through the sealed hatch Kara could hear raised voices and the whine of a cutting torch.

"Where's the docking release?" Nate said, fear rising in his voice.

"How about that one?" Kara asked, pointing to a large red button that was blinking angrily. "It looks like it wants to be pushed."

"I don't know," Nate said. "Red sometimes means—"
She pressed it anyway, and the sub dropped.

16

The Seaweed Forest

Joe's stomach lurched into his mouth as the submersible plummeted nose first. Through the curved glass windscreen he could see nothing, only blackness. But he could imagine the ocean floor rushing towards them; they wouldn't see it until they smashed into it. He pulled Growly from his pocket, clutching the one-armed bear as tightly as he could.

"Prop controls, prop controls," Nate muttered, his knuckles white on the steering bar. Motors ground but nothing caught; they were still dropping.

Kara clutched his arm. "You need to do something."

"I'm trying!" he screamed.

Joe peered through the porthole beside him, twisting to look above and behind them. He thought he could make out a faint shape circled by lights. Then it was swallowed by the darkness.

"What does this do?" Kara asked and light beams pierced the blackness. Motes of algae rushed by like rain.

"How did you do that?" Nate demanded.

"It's got a little picture of a light on it, see? And, here, does that look like a propeller to you?"

Nate peered down. "Maybe. But I don't want to hit the wrong—"

"You should push it," Joe told them. "You should push it now."

The black was turning to grey up ahead, the headlamps illuminating a landscape of rippled dunes rushing towards them at incredible speed. Nate let out a strangled cry, hitting the button. Joe felt the sub vibrate, the motor sputtering into life. Then the propeller caught, kicking them forward.

Nate tugged on the steering bar and the sub levelled out just inches from the sandy surface, speeding like a torpedo over the watery desert. Joe let out a whoop as gravity slammed him back in his seat.

"Maybe I should drive," Kara told Nate. "I can't be any worse than you."

"I'm getting the hang of it," he protested. "It's like riding a bike."

"Since when do Mariners ride bikes?" Kara asked.

"Hey, look out!"

He twisted the wheel, banking round an angular spire of rock.

"No proximity warning," he said shakily. "The sonar must be on the blink. Though that might be a good thing; at least they can't trace our pings."

"Our *what*?" Kara asked.

"Submarines navigate by sound waves. The *Kraken* could track them."

"So we're blind?" Joe put in.

"Not completely. We'll just have to stay low and slow. Keep our eyes peeled and hope we don't crash into anything."

"Great," Kara said. "Sounds like a plan."

Around them the rolling expanse of shallow dunes was broken by patterns of dark stone. Joe saw schools of fish darting into the light, their silver scales flashing. Many-legged creatures scattered for cover, and in the distance he saw a huddle of straight-sided rocks that looked almost man-made. Could this be the remains of a sunken town, a city rich in salvage? No, they were too far out; this must always have been ocean.

Suddenly something slammed against the windscreen, leaving a trail of brown slime. Nate jerked back on the throttle as a shape loomed towards them: a slender rope weaving in the current and another beyond it. The sub brushed past and Joe heard slippery fronds scraping the side.

"Just what we need," Nate said bitterly. In the twin beams they could see an entire forest of undulating wrack, the stems as tall as ships' masts. "Hang on, I'll bring us round."

"Can't we go through?" Kara asked. "They're just plants."

"They'll muddy up the screen. Or wrap round the propeller. I don't fancy going out to unclog it, do you?"

The sub turned, trunks thudding against the hull. "You really are getting better, aren't you?" Kara asked as they broke free of the kelp. "I take it all b——"

"What's that?" Joe asked, pointing. "Is it a light?"

There was a glow up ahead, drifting down towards them.

"Some deep-sea fish are bioluminescent," Nate said. "But I don't know if..."

There was a sudden spark and Nate drew back, shaking his head. "Oh no," he said, twisting the wheel as hard as he could. "Oh no, no. Hold tight."

There was a sudden, terrible noise and white light flooded the cabin. The sub tipped violently. Clouds of sand scoured the starboard portholes, slamming them back into the forest of weeds. A siren sounded and red lights began to flash across the console.

"What's happening?" Kara asked as Nate fought for control.

"He's found us," he said, slamming the steering bar forward. The motors whined as they picked up speed. "Cortez must have taken the second sub. That was a torpedo blast."

Through the rear porthole Joe could see the lights turning in pursuit. On the control panel in front of Kara a metal grille coughed into life. "Attention, *Marlin*." Cortez's voice rattled from the speakers. "This is the *Dory*. Cut your engines or I'll fire again, and this time it won't be a warning."

Kara jabbed at the comms button. "Leave us alone!"

"You know I can't do that. What's happening is bigger than you, Kara. It's bigger than all of us. So power down or I'll have no choice."

Nate kept his eyes forward, the engine straining as they rocketed into the gloom. Joe saw steep bluffs rising on either side, a stone canyon closing them in. "Can we outrun him?"

Nate shook his head. "Cortez is one of the best pilots in the fleet. I wouldn't stand a chance."

"Hide, then," Kara suggested. "Find a cave, turn off

the lights and lie low."

"D'you know how lucky we'd be to find a cave big enough to steer into? No, we need—"

Light rippled through the cabin as a second torpedo tore into the canyon wall above. Rocks tumbled, slamming into the hull, followed by a rain of rattling pebbles.

"I warned you," Cortez said, his voice backed by a low, insistent chime.

Nate's eyes lit up. "Do you hear that?"

Kara was confused. "Hear what?"

He grabbed her hand. "I've got an idea. But it's risky. Like, really risky."

"Do it."

"We could all be killed."

"I trust you. Do it."

Nate wrenched the wheel and the engine protested, motors screaming as the sub struggled to turn without losing pace. "Back home," he said through gritted teeth, "they used to call this game chicken."

The sub completed its arc and he slammed on the throttle. Up ahead Joe could see the lights of the *Dory*, closing in fast. Nate angled towards it, revving the engine.

"What are you doing?" Cortez demanded. "I told you: I won't hesitate to fire."

"Do we have torpedoes too?" Kara asked, pressing

buttons at random. "Can we shoot back?"

Nate grabbed her hand. "One of those is probably the ejector. You wouldn't get far without a pilot."

Something shot past the windscreen and they heard another explosion behind them. Kara hit the comms. "You missed!" she crowed, shielding her eyes as the lights ahead grew brighter, and still brighter. Joe braced himself. For the briefest moment he saw Cortez's face through two panes of glass, eyes glaring as they closed the gap.

Then the collision came, hard and jarring. The subs scraped together, metal grinding on metal. Kara was thrown from her seat but Nate kept hold of the wheel, steadying himself. He reached up, tapping buttons as fast as he could. The sub was plunged into darkness.

"Now we just have to hope we don't run into the sides."

Beams of white light strobed across the starboard portholes as the *Dory* banked behind them. Joe saw the canyon wall looming closer. "Go left!" he shouted, and Nate obeyed.

"Clever trick." Cortez's voice rattled through the speaker. "But I can still see you."

The canyon was lower now, the rippled sand rising to meet them.

"You said we couldn't outrun him," said Kara.

"We don't have to," Nate told her as something struck

the windscreen, screeching along the side. This time he didn't stop but leant hard on the throttle, pressing on into the forest of weeds. The darkness deepened and Joe sank into his seat, the din of countless impacts clattering around him. Then Nate cut the power and they were adrift. The submersible slid smoothly through the tangle of trunks. Gradually they lost momentum, gliding down until they bumped on to the ocean bed.

"That ought to do it," he said, and mopped his brow.

"Won't he follow us?" Kara asked. Through the starboard porthole they could see the lamps of Cortez's sub cutting razor-fine shafts through the wrack.

"He can't," Nate explained. "Cortez must not have recharged the *Dory* after he took her out two nights ago. That was a low power alarm; in a few minutes he'll be forced to the surface and we'll make a run for it."

Kara beamed. "You saved us. I don't believe it." And she planted a kiss on his cheek.

Nate blushed to his roots. "Something could still go wrong. We could get a clog in the propeller, or one of those blasts might have done damage we can't see. They could drop depth charges, or—"

Kara put her hand on his mouth. "Stop talking."

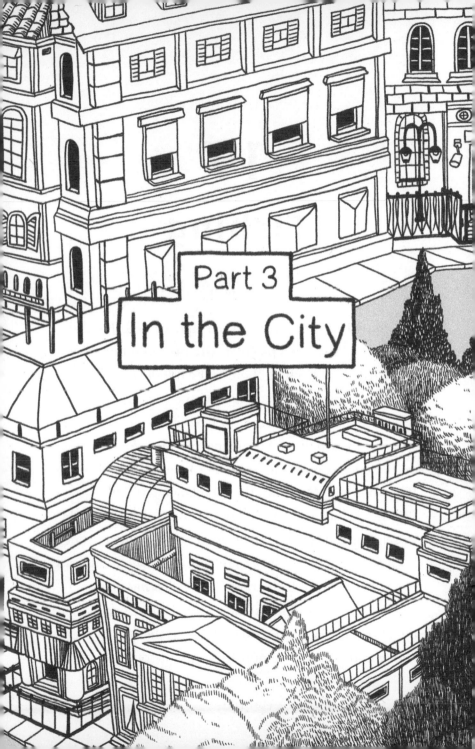

Part 3

In the City

17

Fishing

Joe dipped his line in the water and waited. He didn't have a real lure, just a piece of wire twisted round a lump of algae bread. Even out here in the middle of the ocean, he doubted any fish would find it especially appetising.

The *Marlin* rocked beneath him, its sleek silver body steadied by a pair of branching side fins. Joe crouched on the curved roof, the metal hot beneath his bare feet. It was a bright, hazy day, the sun glancing off the flat sea. But the skyline was empty; there was no sign of another vessel. And it had been that way since sunrise, when they'd been forced to the surface to replenish the solar batteries. As far as they could tell no one was following them.

They'd stayed hidden in the seaweed forest, watching as the *Dory*'s headlamps broke off towards the surface. Kara had feared a trick to tempt them into the open, but Nate had insisted – the longer they stayed, the more danger they were in. They'd gone barely half a mile before his fears were proved right. They'd heard a terrible roar, and looked back to see the jungle of wrack blazing with an unearthly, almost beautiful light. Then the shock wave had hit them, buffeting the little craft as they sped away.

"Those were depth charges," Nate had said afterwards. "He's really got it in for you."

"For *us*," Kara had reminded him.

Joe could hear them again now, strained voices drifting up through the open hatch. The initial relief had given way to bickering as the reality of their situation sank in.

"From where I think we were," Kara was saying, "London should be sort of up, on the right."

"You mean north-east," Nate said. "That's the way we've been going. But we don't know how far south or west we were to begin with, because we didn't think to look at a map."

"Well, I was busy being locked in one of your torture cages," Kara pointed out. "Don't you have charts on that computer thing of yours?"

"It only works when there's a database to link into. I don't even know why I brought it." Nate sighed. "We were supposed to memorise sea lanes at the Academy but I was too busy drawing Aquaboy comics on my oceanography textbook. I can't even navigate by the stars."

"It's day," Kara pointed out.

"I realise that," Nate growled. "I'm just saying they were right, Cane and the others. I'm not a real Mariner. I couldn't tie a reef knot to save my life. I try to enjoy being at sea but I feel sick, like, all the time. And now I've betrayed my own people and run off with a pair of mudfoots."

"Don't be daft, you haven't betrayed them," Kara said. "You said it yourself, if the Mariner High Council knew what Cortez was up to they'd arrest him. He's the one who isn't a real Mariner, not you. Now pass me a fish cake."

"We had the last two for breakfast. From here it's seaweed chips or nothing."

"Wow. We really are in trouble."

Joe got to his feet, the wire twitching in his hands. A silver shape darted into the shadow of the sub, inspecting his blob of bread. He tightened his grip, spreading his feet for balance. He could see the fish now, a good-sized sea bass, thrashing as the hook bit in. He braced himself, jerking the line in steady motions. The fish broke the surface, panicked eyes staring up as Joe gave another tug.

Then he became aware of a mass in the water,

a darkness rising through the sun-dappled sea. Sunlight glittered on something white and jagged. A gaping mouth yawned up at him, the water rolling white as the surface broke.

The wire sheared in two as razor-sharp jaws closed on the wriggling fish. Joe fell hard, feeling something snap as he dropped on his backside. The sub rocked as the shark curved alongside, tail flicking lazily. Joe saw a dorsal fin slicing through the still water.

"What's going on?" Kara poked her head through the hatch, making him jump. "Did something hit us?"

"It was n-nothing," Joe managed. "I think I've done enough fishing for today."

Trembling, he reached into his back pocket. Growly's other arm had broken off when he fell, leaving a sort of furry tube with legs. *Poor bear*, he thought. *Maybe I can glue you.*

Kara climbed the ladder, scanning the horizon. "We've decided we're lost. I've really made a mess of things, haven't I?"

Joe shook his head. "I'm the one who messed up. You tried to warn me what Cortez was like. I should've trusted you a bit more and him a bit less."

Kara laughed. "You like people, Joe. It's one of the reasons I love you."

Joe blushed. "People are OK." He leant against her, feeling her arms round his neck. "Listen, though, I've been thinking. I know we have to go back to the Shanties. Someone has to warn them. But maybe when it's all over we can go somewhere else. Somewhere better."

"You could come to Frisco with me," Nate said, climbing up beside Kara. "I think you'd like it."

"Um, no thanks," Kara said. "I've had quite enough of Mariners for one... Hey, what's that?"

She pointed, shielding her eyes. As a cloud passed over the sun Joe could make out a dark speck against the horizon, a haze of smoke in the air above it. "It's a ship," he said, jumping to his feet and peeling off his shirt, waving it over his head. "Hey! Over here!"

"Wait," Nate said. "What if it's one of ours? Or what if it's fuel pirates? I don't want to end up some pirate's galley slave."

"And I don't want to starve to death out here," Kara objected.

The speck grew larger as it chugged towards them. Nate ducked inside and a moment later Joe saw the sub's headlamps flashing on and off. He waved his shirt again, laughing when he saw an answering beam from the approaching ship. Soon they heard the clatter of engines, and he could make out a rust-patterned prow and a hold piled with scrap metal and machine parts.

"Ahoy," a voice called. "What's your game?"

A man leant out of the rickety cabin; he had ruddy cheeks and a shaggy white beard.

"We need rescue!" Kara shouted. "We have to get to London!"

The trawler drew alongside, the junkman eyeing them suspiciously. "What are you, Mariners? You're dressed like Mariners."

"We escaped from them," Kara explained. "We have to get to the Shanties; it's important."

He squinted. "I'm headed the other way, I'm afraid. I could take you to New Marseille, but my missus'll have my head if I don't flog this salvage to the Frenchies."

"She'll be dead before you get back," Kara said.

The junkman drew back. "Is that a threat?"

"She didn't mean it like that," Joe said hurriedly. "It's just really important we get home."

The old sailor shrugged. "Well, tough luck," he said, revving the throttle. "Try being more polite."

Joe felt Kara's hand tighten on his shoulder. There had to be something they could do, something they could say. Suddenly it came to him.

"Wait!" he called out. "This submersible. How much d'you think it's worth?"

18
The Plan

Kara could smell the Shanties before she could see them, a heavy reek of oil and fish and human waste rolling in on the evening breeze. The water turned from blue to brown, the battered old tugboat cutting through a sump of filth and faeces. She knew it was disgusting, this Stain on the living ocean. But still she felt her spirits lift as the Wall materialised through the heat haze, the jagged shapes of concrete blocks rising from the chemical smog. She was home.

They'd hidden below decks as the ship passed through the outer security cordon, listening breathlessly as the old junkman radioed the officers on duty, explaining how he'd suffered a block in his fuel line and had to turn back for repairs. The *Marlin* bobbed behind with its ballast tanks flooded, just the tail fin poking above the water. Nate hadn't been happy about handing it over, but he'd agreed it was the only way. This time tomorrow the junkman would be rich. If he wasn't dead.

They chugged through the Cut and into the harbour, motors grinding down as he hunted for a berth. Through a zigzag maze of cranes and masts Kara could see the fence and the security turrets, and beyond them the teeming expanse of the Pavilion. There was nothing to stop them walking straight into the Zoo, demanding to see Lieutenant Singh and telling him everything. But he'd failed to protect them last time, and anyway she didn't think he was high-ranking enough to affect anything. There was no sense talking to anybody but the man at the top, and there was only one way she could think to get to him. Yes, her plan was good; it would work. She was almost certain.

The tug drew in beside a row of quayside storehouses and the old man kicked out the gangplank. "Down you go."

"You shouldn't stay here," Joe said, pausing at the top. "You should take your wife and leave."

The junkman frowned. "You're serious? You really think the Mariners are coming?"

"Armed and in force," Kara said.

He scratched his chin. "Well, I suppose I should say

good luck to you. Now get off my boat."

They passed the harbour fence and struck out across the Pavilion, joining the flood of people pouring from the Gullet. It was a giddy feeling being home, the frantic bustle wrapping round Kara like a noisy, comforting blanket. They'd only been gone a few days but it felt like half a lifetime.

Nate walked with his shoulders hunched and his shirt pulled up over his nose. "Are you OK?" Kara asked as they reached the Boardwalk. "I don't think anyone'll recognise you, if that's what you're worried about."

"It's the smell," he hissed. "Every time I breathe I think I'm going to be sick. And everyone's so dirty. Look at that guy, he looks like he hasn't washed in a year."

Kara shrugged. "Probably longer. We can't all afford showers, and what were those bristly things called? Teethbrushes."

She led them north over sturdy steel-frame bridges and between tall well-maintained towers. Joe was so exhausted that they'd almost reached the warehouse before he realised where they were heading. "Hey," he said, his eyes widening. "I thought we were going home!"

"Not right away," Kara said. "Listen, before you get excited. I've got a plan. It'll work. But we need this woman's help."

"But she's a criminal," Joe complained. "She tricked us last time; what makes you think she won't do it again?"

"Because we know something important," Kara said. "And when we tell her about it she's going to be so mad she'll do anything we say."

Maura Glass's response was exactly as Kara had predicted; she smashed her glass down so hard it cracked, the colour rising in her cheeks. "How dare they?" she hissed. "The Shanties are *mine*."

The guard on the gate had recognised them right away, marching them through to the artificial beach where Maura waited, a frilly drink in one hand and a loaded pistol in the other. She'd pointed it at Kara, demanding to know where they'd been and where Redeye was, and how she could track him down and murder him for making her look a fool. Kara had explained everything, and as the tale unfolded Maura's eyes had narrowed to slits, then widened again as she realised the implications of Cortez's plan.

"First they shoot up my home, now they threaten my livelihood," she spat, laying her pistol on the table. "The Shore Boys have run the Shanties for fifty years. Those government boys might control things inside the Wall but out here I'm queen and prime minister rolled into one."

"We don't know exactly what he's planning for the Shanties," Kara said, "but we know Redeye's going after this back door."

"Yes, there were always rumours," Maura mused. "A secret passage under the Wall so the ministers could escape in times of trouble. I assumed it was a myth."

"It's real," Kara said. "Redeye's going to go through it and blow up the government or something."

"But what about MetCo?" Maura asked. "There are hundreds of armed cops inside the City."

"Redeye will have thought of that," Joe put in. "Maybe he's going to murder Mr Remick too."

Maura nodded. "You might be right. MetCo's central offices are at Parliament, so he'll be right there waiting for them. And MetCo couldn't operate without Remick; he makes all the decisions."

Kara bit her lip. She had a question to ask, but she wasn't sure what Maura's reaction would be. "How well do you know him? Remick, I mean."

Maura's head tilted, surprise overwhelming her anger. "What makes you think I know him?"

Kara blanched. "Well, in the Pavilion, while everyone was shooting, you told MetCo not to fire at you and they didn't. You hardly ever hear about Shore Boys being arrested. And it just makes sense. If I was a crime boss,

I'd make a deal with the police so they'd leave me alone."

Maura studied her for a long, silent moment. Then her face cracked into a broad grin. "I'd better keep an eye on you," she cackled. "You'll be after my job in a few years."

Kara blushed. "No, thanks."

"It was my late husband who brokered the deal," Maura explained, "back when MetCo were just another private security firm. It's a simple arrangement – they look the other way and Remick gets a quarter share of our profits. It's a lot of money, but it's worth it. He's never let us down."

"So you could get in to see him?" Kara asked. "Make sure he knows what's coming?"

Maura shook her head. "I've never actually met the man. That was part of the deal: no direct contact, nothing that could be traced back. He's a government employee; the ministers could take away MetCo's contract like that." She snapped her fingers.

"So how would you get hold of him, if you absolutely had to?" Kara asked.

"I guess I'd send someone to his office in Parliament," Maura said. "Carrying a message that only Remick would understand. But it'd have to be someone with no obvious ties to the Shore Boys. Someone they wouldn't suspect."

"Like a kid?" Kara asked. "Maybe even a kid that

Remick would recognise?"

"Yes, that'd be perfect," Maura said, nodding. "Wait, you mean you?"

"Who else?" Kara asked. "Remick saw me at the Zoo. You tell me the right words to make him listen, and I tell him everything I just told you. All we'd need are passes to get inside the City."

Maura sipped her cocktail thoughtfully. "You know, it might work. I could have the passes made up overnight. Then you warn Remick, I round up my Shore Boys, and when these kelp-eaters turn up we drive them back into the sea." She frowned. "But you can't go inside the Wall looking like a bunch of little Mariners. Come on, I bet we can find you something a bit more suitable."

The next morning, Joe awoke to the cry of seabirds. For a moment he was back on the *Neptune*, cocooned in soft blue warmth. But when he opened his eyes he saw grimy brick walls and a rotted wooden floor, and smelled the reek of sweat and Selkie. They were in a stone storeroom deep inside the Shore Boys' warehouse stacked with packing crates and rusty camp beds. He wondered if this was where the brewery workers slept when they were too weak or too drunk to get home.

He could hear voices in the adjoining corridor – Kara

192

and Mrs Glass talking low. A moment later Kara stepped back in, her face reddening when she saw that he was awake.

"Everything all right?" Joe asked.

She smoothed down the fur-trimmed peach dress that Maura had selected from her stock of stolen goods. "Fine. I just feel a bit daft wearing this."

"Mrs Glass said they were the latest fashions." Nate sat up on his bunk, resplendent in a blue herringbone jacket with crimson lapels. "Personally I think we look pretty nifty."

"Well, I feel like a Little Candy doll," Kara muttered resentfully.

Out in the courtyard the Shore Boys were starting to assemble, checking their ammunition clips and strapping on their bulletproof armour. "I'm sending a squad to the Pavilion," Maura explained. "They'll report back if they see anything suspicious, like a giant black submarine."

Kara handed Joe a sheet of paper and a pencil. "We thought it might be useful if you could copy out everything you remember about Elroy's map."

He bent over the glass table, sticking out his tongue as he sketched the outer circle and the wiggly lines, marking the cross where he thought it should go. "The words as well," Kara said. "Wellington, and the rest."

Joe jotted them down – *Sun four, six down, news, Wellington.* Nate took the computer tablet from his pocket and held it over the map. There was a flash and a perfect image appeared on the screen. "You won't need that," Joe said. "I can remember how it goes."

Nate blushed. Kara opened her mouth and shut it again.

"Tell him," Maura said. "He deserves to know."

Joe was confused. "Tell me what?"

Kara knelt awkwardly. "Joe, the thing is—" She broke off, biting her lip. "Look, you can't come with us. Inside the Wall. It's too risky. I told Maura to make just two passes, for me and Nate."

Joe looked at the Mariner boy. "But I... But he..."

"He needs to be there," Kara insisted. "He can help me convince Remick, tell him stuff only a Mariner would know."

"But so could I!" Joe insisted. "I could convince him too!"

"What if we're too late and we run into Redeye?" Kara asked. "All he'd have to do is point a gun at you and I'd do anything he said. No, you stay with Maura. Tell her everything you know about Cortez so the Shore Boys have the best chance to fight him."

"But that's boring!" Joe protested. "I'm not a kid – I

fooled Cortez and I got you out of that cage. You wouldn't be here without me. This isn't fair."

"I know," Kara admitted. "I'm sorry. But it's the way it has to be."

Joe turned away, so angry that his hands were shaking. He was the one Elroy gave the map to; he was the one Redeye came after. And now he wouldn't get to see inside the Wall. He wouldn't get to save the Shanties. *That must be it*, he thought. *Kara just wants all the glory for herself. She's always been selfish.*

He heard them saying their farewells to Maura, followed by the creak of the big iron gate. He took a deep breath, trying to stop the tears from falling.

"She did the right thing, you know," Maura said, touching his arm gently. "Partly because my Shore Boys can keep you safe. And partly because I have another use for you."

Joe looked up, surprised.

"Kara's plan is smart," Maura explained, "but what if something goes wrong? What if she's arrested at the barrier, or Remick refuses to see her? This is too important to risk everything on a single throw. I need a backup plan, and for that I need you."

She gestured to a small band of Shore Boys standing by the far wall, their bald-headed lieutenant striding along the line. Joe recognised him from last time – Zuma, was that his name?

"Those are my very best men," Maura explained. "My crack squad. But they're not going to the Pavilion with the others. They're taking a boat to the Badlands to look for this back door, and our old friend Redeye. I thought I'd go along in case they find him. You know the Mariners, and you know the map. Why don't you join us?"

19
Oxford Street

The air inside the Gullet was clammy and stifling, condensation collecting on the low ceiling and trickling into drainage grates set into the black concrete floor. The Shanty folk trudged wearily in their brown uniforms, their faces sallow as daylight gave way to a harsh neon glare. Kara could feel them eyeing her, wondering what a girl in a dress like that was doing in a place like this.

Nate straightened his tie, peering uncomfortably at the roof. "I can't help thinking about all that concrete up there," he whispered. "What if it falls on us?"

"The Wall's stood for decades," Kara reassured him. "I doubt it's going to fall down today."

The crowd slowed and she saw brightness up ahead – not sunlight, but a row of strip-bulbs. A steel security barrier blocked the tunnel, fronted with reinforced glass.

MetCo patrolmen lined the walls, their rifles shouldered, their dogs snarling on the leash.

Kara swallowed and swiped her forged entry pass, waiting for an alarm to shriek and cuffs to clamp round her wrists. But the sentries didn't even glance her way as the gate swung open and she stepped through, Nate close on her heels.

Soon they could see light in the distance, real daylight this time, streaming through the Gullet's mouth. The workers picked up the pace, sweeping them along. Above the chatter Kara could hear other, stranger sounds: an irregular nasal honk and a growl like outboard motors. She smelled sweat and chem-oil, but cutting through it all was a sweet, fresh fragrance like nothing she recognised.

Nate grabbed her hand as they were driven from the tunnel into a large cobblestone plaza swarming with people. Slender trees grew on either side and above them rose the Wall, vast and white, curving inward. *I'm inside*, Kara thought. *And it's beautiful*.

The workers kept up a steady pace, crossing towards a rank of bright red two-storey automobiles parked beside a busy four-lane roadway. But it wasn't the vehicles that drew Kara's attention, or the imposing glass-and-stone buildings that rose tier upon tier. It was the expanse of open ground beyond the road, a rolling carpet of jewelled green like something from a dream.

"Grass," she said, savouring the word in her mouth. The park sparkled with morning dewdrops, dotted with wildflowers and shady spreading trees. Kara felt Nate watching her and blushed. "Hey, it's not my fault I've never seen the stuff before."

He frowned apologetically. "Just try not to gawp. We're supposed to belong here, remember?"

A horn blared and Kara looked up to see a sleek blue jalopy veering up the road towards the plaza. A young man in an enormous three-cornered hat leant from the window, waving at the Shanty workers queuing for their transport. "Hey, rats!" he shouted. "Need a wash?"

He flung three small projectiles and the workers scattered as the balloons exploded, showering them with water. "No need to thank me!" the boy hooted as the car sped away.

The Shanty folk stood, silently dripping. One of them glowered at Kara, red-faced with embarrassment. *No*, she wanted to shout, *can't you see? I'm like you, but in disguise.*

"He's one of the people we came to save?" Nate asked. "Maybe we shouldn't bother."

Kara sighed. "We're here for the Shanties," she said. "Come on, let's find this Parliament place. Maura gave me money for a taxicab, whatever that is."

"The black ones, I think."

Nate stuck out his hand and a dark vehicle pulled up beside them, the rear door swinging open. He hopped inside but Kara froze, the cab vibrating before her like a hunched animal.

"It won't hurt you," Nate promised. "Think of it like a boat with wheels."

She gritted her teeth and climbed over the threshold, and the cab peeled away.

"Parliament please," Nate said.

The driver nodded. "Right you are."

Kara wondered what part of the Shanties he was from; all she could see was a tuft of grey hair beneath a peaked cap. She felt her stomach tighten as they picked up speed, curving round a stone arch patterned with men and horses before turning into a long street with stone buildings on both sides. The windows were heaped with gadgets and garments, gold-trimmed furniture and strings of silver jewellery. City folk marched from shop to shop, laughing and spending. Their clothes were dazzling, their skin gleamed. Their Shanty-born servants struggled behind with overflowing bags.

Kara had known it would be different in here, that people would be clean and healthy and rich. But the scale of it was still mind-boggling; all these shops, all this money, all this *stuff*.

"Impressive, ain't it?" the cabbie asked, glancing at her in the mirror. "People come from all around the world to shop on Oxford Street. You can get electronics from the Andes, spices from the Kush, suits and boots from the mills up north. Where are you kids from? I'm guessing you're not local."

"Cal— er, Canada," Nate said. "Our Dad's here on a trade delegation."

"Maple syrup, right?" the cabbie grinned. "Never tasted it myself but I hear it's delicious."

"Doesn't it make you feel angry?" Kara asked before she could stop herself. "I mean, these people have so much and you … you're not…"

The driver eyed her, trying to figure out why a Canadian girl in expensive clothes had the same accent he did. Then he just shrugged. "The way I see it, you make the best of what you've got. They got born lucky, I didn't. But I've a decent job. Back in the Shanties… You've heard of the place, right? The Shanties?"

Kara nodded quickly.

"Well, some of our neighbours hate the folks in here, say they're keeping us down, keeping us poor. I can see their point; when my kids can't have proper shoes or the wife can't get medicine for her arthritis, I'll admit it's hard. But this is the way things are. And at least we're better off than those stinking Mariners, right?"

Nate forced a chuckle. "Good point."

Kara hunkered down, staring resentfully out of the window. The cab slowed, overtaking a two-wheeled cart hooked to a bicycle. Three men in suits lounged inside, sipping drinks as the driver pedalled furiously, sweat pouring down her back. An old woman hobbled past, strung with so many gold chains that her back was bent. A pigtailed boy followed, taking one bite from a candy apple before dropping it in the gutter.

Then for the briefest second Kara saw a dark shape in the midst of it all, a tall shadow stalking through the crowd. She gasped, pressing her face to the glass. No, it was impossible. She was tired and spooked; it wasn't surprising that her brain would start conjuring phantoms.

"See someone you know?" the driver asked. "You'd think in a city this size you'd never run into anyone, but I'm forever—"

"Stop!" Kara shouted, a wave of cold dread running down her spine. "I see him. I really see him."

Redeye strode along the pavement, silhouetted in the glare from the shop windows. His Mariner robes were gone; he wore a tailored suit and carried a steel briefcase, a patch covering his artificial eye. Behind him strode two more Mariners, broad-shouldered Pavel and another man with a pinched face that Kara half recognised.

"We were wrong," she gasped, reaching for the handle. "We were wrong about all of it!"

Nate grabbed her wrist as the cab slammed to a halt. "What are you doing?"

"Don't you see?" Kara asked, shoving the door open. "If Redeye's already here that means I was wrong about the map, and about the back door. I have to follow him or we'll never know what they're really up to."

"You're not going anywhere without paying," the cabbie said, reaching through the partition to grab Nate's sleeve.

Kara backed out apologetically. "I'll come back. I'm really sorry."

Nate's eyes widened. "Kara, you can't!"

But she was already gone, horns blaring as she flung herself across the street. She kicked off her shoes, watching them tumble into the road. The peach dress was tight round her knees so she paused on the pavement, ripping the seam. People stopped to watch, some laughing, others shaking their heads. Kara shoved past them.

Looking ahead, she thought for a heart-stopping minute that she'd lost them. Had Redeye seen her and ducked into one of the shops? But no, there he was, striding through the colourful crowd like a shark in a school of guppies. Kara dodged towards him, knowing she didn't have a plan. Should she cry "Mariner"? No, that would only spark a stampede, giving Redeye the chance to escape. For now all she could do was keep him in sight. Hopefully he wouldn't look back.

He looked back.

Kara tried to duck but it was too late. Redeye's good eye widened in disbelief and he gestured to his fellow Mariners, all three quickening their pace. Kara pushed through, feeling like a boat in a current, nudged this way and that but holding her course.

The Mariners turned into a narrow street; there were fewer people here and the shops were a little less garish. Redeye glanced back without slowing. "I like your dress. You look almost like a girl."

"I like the patch," Kara called back. "You look almost like a person."

Redeye laughed. "You were always quick. Let's see how quick you really are."

And he bolted off down the street, tossing his briefcase to Pavel.

Kara followed instinctively, cutting an arc round the other Mariners. Redeye had already widened the gap, his long legs pumping. She shoved through a herd of bewildered shoppers, accidentally elbowing one into the street. Horns blared but she kept running.

They emerged into a pedestrian square, tourists swarming like butterflies. Chairs were arranged in the sun and there was a strong smell, like chicory but better. *Real coffee*, Kara realised. Redeye bounded over the cobbles, increasing his lead. But then a gaggle of sightseers burst suddenly from a building, milling out into the sunlight. Redeye plunged into them and Kara heard furious protests, voices asking if he was blind or just stupid. He growled and shoved through.

Kara skirted the group, moving to cut him off. Along the side of the building ran an alley leading to a small yard – she saw tables inside with people seated round them. Redeye ducked in without looking and Kara followed, praying he'd made a mistake.

Her heart lifted. The yard was a dead end with high walls on all four sides.

Redeye turned, trapped. "I don't know how you found me but I'm on a schedule, Kara. Don't make me hurt you."

She glanced around. "These people might have something to say about a grown man beating up a defenceless little girl."

Redeye laughed. "Have you forgotten where we are? They won't lift a finger."

He lunged, feinting one way then ducking the other, trying to slip by. Kara grabbed his jacket, trying to pull him back. "Whatever you're doing," she said as buttons popped. "It stops here."

Redeye tried to swing at her but his arms were pinned, the material bunching in Kara's fist. Then a voice shouted "Hey!" and she was hauled back, kicking and swiping. An arm locked round her throat, lifting her off the floor. She couldn't see her assailant, just his expensive wristwatch.

Redeye smoothed his jacket, slipping his patch back in place. "She just attacked me," he said, aggrieved. "I've never even seen her before. Hold her – she's stronger than she looks."

Kara tried to speak but the pressure on her neck was too tight. People pressed in for a better look and Redeye took a step back. Kara struggled but it was no use; he tipped her a wink as the crowd closed around him.

"I think she's from the Shanties," her captor said, grunting with the effort of holding her. "She certainly smells like it."

"Probably a common thief," a woman sneered. "Restrain her until the police arrive."

Kara fought, feeling helpless. There was only one thing for it.

Baring her teeth she sunk them into her captor's arm just above his watch. She felt the skin break and heard him howl, dropping her instinctively. Wiping the blood from her mouth she shoved through the startled crowd, fleeing wildly across the square.

20

Parliament

Kara sprinted through the back alleys of London, darting left then right, evading any chance of pursuit. Redeye had vanished, slipping away into the maze of grey stone. But she thought she knew where he was heading, and she was determined to get there first.

As she ran she remembered Colpeper's words that day in Regent's Village. This part of the City really did feel like something out of a history book, a glimpse of the old world before the waters rose. She'd never been much of a reader, but back at the Sisterhood they used to tell stories from before the Tech Age, tales of lamplit terraces and shrouding fog, noble lords and wily thieves. She'd always struggled to picture the places in her imagination, visualising streets of water and carriages with oars. But now the stories came back to her all in a rush – she felt like Olive Twits himself, fleeing through the friendless streets one step ahead of the law.

She came to a corner and peered round. Across the road was a building with a lit awning, the words THE MOUSETRAP emblazoned on it. Kara was perplexed – maybe they kept giant mice inside and people paid to watch them get caught.

"It's a theatre," a voice said, and she turned. Beneath a lamp post stood the largest girl Kara had ever seen. She must have been seven feet tall and at least four wide, her green dress almost spherical as it ballooned around her. Her nose was pointed upward and her accent was so precise it could cut steel. "It's where they show plays."

"I know what a theatre is," Kara said. Then she forced herself to smile. "But thank you."

The girl shrugged her massive shoulders. "Well, I don't know. You're clearly not from around here, wearing tat like that."

Kara blushed, looking down at her torn dress. "But it's the latest fashion."

The girl snorted. "Three years ago, maybe. Perhaps in the provinces those colours are still the rage, but at this year's London parties it is *all* about size." She studied Kara. "Are you lost? I can help if you are – I know these streets like the back of my glove." She held up one silk-covered hand.

Kara frowned. "You … you want to help me?"

The girl yawned. "I'm frightfully bored. My driver's late and I can't go anywhere until he returns, not in these shoes. Where are you trying to go?"

Kara hesitated. "P-Parliament?"

The girl nodded approvingly. "Good. Important place, lots of heritage. You go that way, take a right and … what on earth's the matter?"

Kara shrank back as a MetCo officer emerged from an alley across the street, strolling in their direction. She was trapped – the cop would surely spot her if she tried to run, assuming the girl didn't alert him first.

Then she heard a cough and saw the girl gesturing urgently, holding up the base of her enormous skirt. "Get in," she hissed.

For a moment Kara was too surprised to move. Then she gulped and ducked down, crawling into the cavern of cloth. The hem dropped and she was cocooned in pale green.

The first thing she saw was a pair of boots so ludicrously elevated they were almost stilts. The girl was probably no taller than she was, Kara realised. And no broader either – her stockinged legs were straight and slender. This whole outfit was an illusion, crafted to make her appear much bigger than she was. Kara didn't really understand why, but she had to admit it was impressive.

She could hear voices now, muffled by the material – the girl casual and innocent, the policeman gruff but deferential. She heard footsteps clumping away, then the hem rose once more.

"You can come out."

Kara scrambled free, her face flushed. "Why are you hiding from the police?" the girl asked. "Are you a Mariner? Steady on, you're not going to blow up Parliament are you?"

"I'm not a Mariner," Kara said. "I'm actually trying to stop them."

The girl's eyes widened. "Well, that sounds frightfully exciting. I suppose you'd better run along. I'd come with you, only I can barely move." She drew something from her purse, holding it out. "Here, eat this. It'll keep you going."

Kara took the brightly coloured choc-bar, backing away. "Th-thank you."

"Hang on," the girl called after her. "What's your name so I can tell my friends?"

Kara told her, and the girl looked genuinely startled. "How bizarre. That's my name too."

They stared at one another, and couldn't help laughing.

Then the girl waved her handkerchief and Kara backed away, fleeing along the shadowed street.

She nibbled the bar as she ran, almost gagging on the intense flavour. But she felt a burst of energy as she broke into sunlight, finding herself in a wide thoroughfare with trees lining either side. To her right a giant clock tower rose, capped with pointed steel. Maura had told her to look for it – it had a daft name, Big Bill or something. Beyond it she could see gleaming spires and sloping roofs, Parliament itself. At its back the Wall rose pale and smooth.

Kara kept her head down, hoping no one would notice her torn dress and bare feet. The Houses of Parliament were surrounded by a black steel fence, the gates manned by sentries with rifles slung across their backs. She strode towards the nearest one, remembering the code words Maura had given her. "I'm here to see Alexander Remick," she said, and the guard turned. "Tell him—"

The sentry gasped.

"You!" Kara exclaimed.

Singh had traded his lieutenant's uniform for a blue dress coat and a peaked cap; it didn't suit him, Kara thought. He looked like a grown man in boy's clothes. He stared at her, tugging his moustache. "Kara Jordan, you're alive. But what are you doing here? We're inside the Wall!"

"I've come to warn Mr Remick," Kara said. "The Mariners are coming back."

Singh looked around. "What do you mean? Coming here?"

Kara nodded. "Any minute. So you have to take me to him."

Singh shook his head. "I'm afraid that's impossible. After that mess in the Pavilion the minister told Remick I'd been insubordinate and I got busted down to guard duty. Kara, I'm so sorry I let you down; she had a gun to my head and—"

"I forgive you," Kara said. "But, honestly, Remick will want to see me. You just have to tell him to remember his friends in low places."

Singh's eyes narrowed. "What does that mean? Kara, what are you up to?"

"I'll explain everything, I promise," she said. "Oh, but could you also find out if there's been a boy brought in for not paying his taxi fare? He's not going to be very happy with me."

The black speedboat banked, cutting round the tip of the harbour and into open water. Joe perched on the front bench, Maura's arm round his shoulder. She smelled like flowers and expensive whisky.

Zuma had the wheel, curving expertly between the ships as they entered the Southern Cut. Six black-clad Shore Boys crouched in the back, their rifles across their knees.

"I've never been this way before," Joe said. "I always wanted to, but Kara said it was dangerous."

"And she was right," Maura said. "But we'll protect you."

A heavy peace descended as they moved into the Badlands. Stone towers closed in around them, but these weren't the bustling blocks of the Shanties; there were no walkways down here, and no people either. Few of the buildings rose more than five stories, their concrete tops cragged and crumbling, like bad teeth biting at the sky. And it went on for miles, Joe knew. South London was an uncharted wasteland.

Zuma eased back on the throttle, standing upright with his eyes on the water. Joe saw stone peaks below the surface, waiting to snag an unwary vessel. Seagulls lifted into the air, crying a warning.

"Keep as close as you can to the Wall," Maura said. "And look for anything unusual."

"Whole place is unusual," Zuma grunted.

Ahead of them a block had subsided completely,

a concrete landslide sloping into the sea. On the slabs lay a family of fat brown seals, yawning as the speedboat approached. Joe could feel the stillness around them, oppressive and somehow watchful. He thought he saw movement in a high window but it could have been anything: a bird, a stray dog. He shivered and Maura gave him a squeeze. "Do you think we're on the right track, Joe?"

He looked at the scrap of paper in his hands. "The 'x' is here. So we must be close."

Zuma powered the motor down. "Don't matter no way. We can't go further."

Joe couldn't tell what had caused the collapse; it looked like a bomb had gone off, though it was probably just decades of erosion. Ahead was a mountain of debris where twenty or more buildings had tumbled into one another, blocking the waterway completely.

"Could go south and round," Zuma suggested. "But could be far."

"We're close enough," Maura said. "Take us in, we'll continue on foot."

The Wall filled the horizon, rising from the rubble. At its base Joe could see the Boardwalk jutting just above the water. *So it's true*, he thought. *It really does run all the way round.*

Suddenly Zuma ducked, cutting the engine dead. "Mariner," he whispered, drawing his pistol.

Maura peered up cautiously. "Looks like he's waiting for somebody."

"Shoot to kill?" Zuma asked, screwing a silencer to the barrel. Maura nodded.

Joe took her arm. "Do you have to? He might know something useful."

"And if all we do is wound him, he'll scream and we'll lose our advantage. Zuma, do it."

The big man took aim, squeezing the trigger almost gently. Then he dropped back into his seat, turning the key as though nothing had happened. Joe shuddered as the engine fired up.

"We're trying to save a lot of lives here, Joe," Maura said. "Remember that."

Joe nodded, but he wasn't convinced. Maura was on their side for now, but he didn't think she cared that much about saving people. She was perfectly happy to exploit Shanty folk in her brewery, and probably in other ways too. She was only here because the Mariners threatened her business.

The Mariner skiff was moored beside a natural beach formed from slabs of smashed concrete, the dead man lying face down in the shallows. Zuma climbed out of the speedboat, hooking the painter round an exposed steel bar.

Maura settled back on the front bench, looking up at the Wall. "Someone needs to stay in case Redeye shows up," she said. "And climbing over rubble isn't exactly my forte. O'Toole, take two men and go west towards the harbour. Zuma, you and the others head east. Report back if you find anything. Me and Joe will keep watch."

Joe thought about arguing, but a little part of him was relieved. He was glad he'd finally seen the Badlands, but that didn't mean he had to go off exploring in it. Even on a sunny day this was the spookiest place he'd ever been.

The Shore Boys clambered up towards the Boardwalk, their dark figures outlined against the white of the Wall. Maura settled back with her feet on the dashboard, closing her eyes. "I'm just going to catch forty winks," she said. "Wake me if the shooting starts."

Joe crouched in the boat and listened to the silence.

"I saw them," Kara insisted. "There are Mariners inside the Wall. Why won't you listen to me?"

Remick stopped in the stone corridor, his red face inches from hers, his shaggy hairpiece quivering. "You

217

watch your tone, missy. I know what you think you saw. I just don't believe it."

He strode on, shoving through the bustle of uniformed cops and office staff who crowded the arched hallway. Many of them were hauling boxes and crates, and through the window Kara could see a truck being loaded. MetCo's offices in the Houses of Parliament were undoubtedly impressive, but why was everything so hectic? She didn't have time to worry about it.

"What about the map?" she asked, hurrying at Remick's heels. "Won't you at least give it a proper look?"

Nate held up his computer tablet, displaying Joe's drawing. He'd been brought from a holding cell moments before, shaken but unharmed – the cabbie had turned him in when he couldn't pay, but Singh had managed to secure his release. The former lieutenant followed close behind, tugging at his moustache and wearing the face of a man who might've made a terrible mistake.

"I don't need to look at it," Remick barked. "Childish scribbles and nonsense."

Kara grabbed his sleeve. "Maura Glass trusted us," she hissed. "You should too."

Remick's face turned scarlet and he struggled to speak. Then he seized Kara by her fur-lined collar and shoved her across the hallway, slamming her through a door into an empty reception room with wooden panels on the walls.

"Don't you ever speak that name to me," he said in a fierce whisper. "Never, do you understand?"

Kara nodded breathlessly and Remick let go, straightening her collar as Nate and Singh entered.

"Now, I'm already late," he said. "But let me take a moment to explain why your story makes no sense. First, you say John Cortez is coming in a submarine. How does he get past the security cordon? We have boats every ten miles, and between each one are fifty electronic sensors sunk into the seabed. If just one was triggered, alarms would ring across the network and thirty naval cruisers would converge on his location."

"He said something about a friend inside the City," Kara said. "Maybe it's even one of your own people. That would explain how Redeye got an entry pass."

Remick bristled. "MetCo officers are trained to be absolutely loyal. I know each of them personally; none could be capable of this treachery. Singh, back me up."

"It's unlikely," Singh admitted. "But people are people."

Remick shook his head. "No, I refuse to believe it. And besides, no single man has the authority this would require. To smuggle someone into the City, access the back door *and* shut down the cordon? Are you saying they persuaded a whole group of my officers to betray me?"

"So the back door does exist?" Kara said. "I was right about that?"

"That's classified," Remick said. "And even if it did, it would be heavily guarded."

Singh cleared his throat awkwardly. "Sir, if it makes any difference, Kara never struck me as a liar. I'm not saying you have to believe every word, but it might be worth taking a few small measures. Double the harbour sentries. Dispatch more ships to the cordon. And send men to patrol the streets for this Redeye. I can give them a description."

Remick's eyes narrowed. "And I suppose you're volunteering to lead them as well? No, I won't allow you to use this … confused child to further your own pitiful career." He turned back to Kara. "So then, what am I to do with you? I can't have you running about causing a panic. No, it'll have to be the work farms. No one there will listen, and it won't matter if they do. Lieutenant, your handcuffs."

Kara's throat tightened. If they took her away, Joe would be left in the Shanties alone, not knowing what had happened to her. She backed away as Remick glared at Singh.

"Restrain them or you're fired."

Singh hesitated, but only for a moment. He unclipped two sets of handcuffs from his belt, locking one round Kara's wrists. "I'm sorry," he whispered. "Again."

Remick crossed to the door. "Put them in separate cells and fill in the transfer forms. I'll check later; don't think I won't. You're on thin ice with me, Singh. Don't fall through."

He slammed the door and Singh sighed, mopping his brow. "That could've gone better."

"You can't send us away," Kara protested. "You believe me, I know you do. Cortez is coming and we're the only ones who can stop him."

"Why wouldn't he listen?" Nate wondered. "It was like he didn't want to."

"The boss can be stubborn," Singh admitted. "But he was right about the back door. I had that assignment myself, guarding the access tunnel on Sub Level Four. No one's getting through; the steel's this th—"

"Wait," Nate broke in. "Go back. Did you say something about Sub Four?"

"Right," Singh said. "On the basement levels. But, trust me, there are men on duty day and night."

"Joe's map," Kara said. "*Sub*, not *sun*! We have to go down there."

Singh laughed, exasperated. "Kara, don't be crazy,

that's a highly restricted—"

With a clunk the lights went out. There was a scream and in the distance they heard the rattle of gunfire. "Too late," Nate said. "They're here."

21

The Badlands

Joe perched in the front of the speedboat, Maura snoring softly beside him. Waves slapped against the hull of the Mariner skiff, the dead man spinning slowly in the water. Seagulls dipped and dived, the seals basked on their island of rock, but Joe couldn't help feeling there was something else here. Something watching him. He yawned, turned and almost jumped out of his skin.

Two green eyes were staring at him above a mouth filled with pointed teeth. White claws gripped the concrete. Joe caught his breath.

"What are you doing out here?" he asked the ginger cat. "Where's your mum?"

The cat eyed him suspiciously then it began to wash, licking its mangy fur with a little pink tongue. Joe could see a line of ribs beneath the piebald skin. "This isn't a good place," he said. "You should come home with me, there's stuff to eat and other cats to play with."

Cautiously he pulled himself up on to the gunwale, swinging his feet over. But the moment he stepped down on to the concrete shore the cat bolted, scurrying to the top of a rubble-strewn slope. There it stopped, watching him resentfully.

Joe gave a sigh and followed, scaling the incline on his hands and feet. The concrete was loose and treacherous, spikes of glass poking through. But there were plants too – little patches of moss and seagrass. He reached the summit and looked around. Below him the boats rocked on the winking waves. But he could see no sign of the Shore Boys; the towers blocked his view in both directions.

He stepped towards the cat, making reassuring noises. The going was smooth, and looking down he realised he was following a makeshift path through the debris. Two blocks had once stood here, many storeys high. Now they were just stumps, leaning together so their shattered tops touched a hundred feet above his head. The path led between them, winding into the darkness.

He stood for a moment, listening. The wind whistled through empty windows and he heard a faint scuffling, like footsteps in the dust.

"Nope," he said to the ginger cat. "Even I'm not stupid

enough to go in there."

But the cat wasn't looking at him. It was staring into the dark space between the buildings, its back arched, its fur on end. Joe looked, and that was when he saw the girl.

She stood alone in the middle of the path, a torn skirt clinging to her legs. In her hand she clutched a doll, just a bundle of rags with a face scrawled on it. She was younger than Joe, maybe six or seven, but so thin it was hard to tell. She had big brown eyes and dirty bare feet.

"Hey," Joe said, taking a step forward. "You live here?"

The girl smiled shyly.

"Do you need help?"

She nodded and rubbed her belly.

"You're hungry?" Joe said. "I don't have anything. I'd share if I did."

"Liar," said a voice and Joe spun round, cursing.

A grey-haired figure in tattered shorts stood blocking his escape. He was young as well, and just as thin as the girl. His eyes were narrow and mean. "What you doing in our blocks?" he asked.

"Nothing," Joe said quickly. "Leaving."

The ragged boy smiled, lips drawing back over cracked teeth. "Not leave. Stay. Be friends."

Hearing a rustle, Joe looked up. A second boy came clambering from one of the broken towers, angling spider-like over the windowsill and dropping to the concrete. Another head poked from the opposite block, followed by another, and another. Tiny figures swarmed out, clambering over the ledges and down the leaning walls, slipping their toes into minute cracks in the brickwork. More emerged from the darkness between the buildings, surrounding Joe and regarding him impassively.

"What you got?" the first boy asked. "What you give?"

Joe patted his pockets. "I've only got this bear," he said, pulling out the plastic figure. "His name's Growly; he's from space or something. But he doesn't have any arms."

The boy glared, and Joe knew that look: hunger, mistrust and jealousy. They'd take whatever he had, and if there was nothing to take they'd take it out on him. So he let the ragged boy draw closer, closer and, as he reached up to take the bear Joe whipped out with his free hand, grabbing him by the wrist and yanking him back. He was tall but skeleton-light, so thin that Joe was able to fit his whole arm round the boy's neck.

"Stop!" he shouted as the others moved in. "I don't want trouble. I just want to leave."

"You a spy?" the first girl demanded, peering up with moon-like eyes. "You from Rubble Kings?"

"I'm not from any gang," Joe said. "I just went the

wrong way."

"Lies," the boy spat, wriggling. "You Rubble King spy. Doorkeepers hate Rubble Kings."

"Doorkeepers?" Joe asked, clinging on. "That's what you call yourselves?"

"Baddest gang in the Badlands," the boy sneered. "You heard of us?"

"No, I just wondered about the name," Joe said. "What door? Wh—"

"Do it, now!" the girl squealed suddenly, her face filled with savage glee.

Joe jerked back too late. Something hard and heavy struck him between the shoulder blades, knocking him to his knees.

A child leant from a high window, a victorious grin on her face. A half-brick lay shattered on the stones.

Before Joe could stand they were all around him, kicking and punching, driving him down. The ragged boy cackled. "What door?" he yelled as his foot slammed into Joe's side. "We show you what door!"

The girl moved in, her eyes gleaming. She held Joe's nose with her fingers, forcing him to open his mouth. Then she shoved her doll inside, jamming the greasy bundle of rags between his teeth. He felt hands round his wrists and ankles, lifting him off his feet.

The ragged boy cackled with glee. "Doorkeepers gonna eat well tonight!"

Two MetCo officers lay spreadeagled on the tiled floor of Sub Level Four staring up at the ceiling. Their guns had been taken, their radios smashed. Behind them a steel door stood wide, dented with bullet holes. Beyond the door was darkness.

Singh knelt, checking their wrists. He shook his head.

"Redeye," Kara said. "Do you believe us now?"

Singh nodded. "We'll go to Mr Remick. We'll prove to him—"

"There's no time," Kara said. "They're heading for the back door. We're the only ones who can stop them."

"Us?" Nate asked. "I mean, I'll come if you want, but I don't think I'll be much—"

"Stop," Kara cut in, facing him. "Who attacked John Cortez with a fire extinguisher? Who piloted that sub to safety?"

"Erm, me?" Nate asked, only half certain.

"Exactly. So stop acting like a coward, because you're not one."

Nate blushed, managing to look frightened, flattered and embarrassed all at once. Singh squeezed his shoulder. "If it makes you feel better, I'm terrified too. But I think she's right; it's down to us now."

Stepping over the bodies, Kara knew she should be just as frightened. But somehow her nerves were steady. She had a job to do and it was more important than anything, even fear.

Beyond the door was a vertical shaft with a steep metal staircase winding down through it. There were lights in the wall and the steps were cold beneath her bare feet.

Nate checked the map as they descended. "The next clue is *six down*. And look, there's a sort of flat bit every time the stairs do a loop. Maybe it means six of those."

"Please tell me you've been counting," Kara said.

"Of course. That's four."

"I see a door," Singh said, peering over the railing. "Two loops down."

The staircase continued, but they stopped at the door. Singh took the handle, but before he could open it Kara held up a hand. "Hang on. I've been thinking."

"That sounds ominous," Nate muttered.

"Redeye doesn't know you're with us," Kara told Singh. "He knows me and Nate have the map and that we're in the City, so if we show up he won't be surprised. But he doesn't know about you."

"What's your point?" he asked.

"I think we should split up," Kara said. "No, listen. Me

and Nate can go on ahead. You follow a little way behind, so if they catch us you can still get the drop on them."

Nate sighed. "So we're bait is what you're saying?"

"If you want to look at it like that."

Singh stepped back. "Makes sense to me. I'll stay close and keep you in sight."

Kara grasped the handle. "Ready?" she asked. "One, two…"

She yanked the door open, springing back with a cry. Singh raised his pistol and Nate pressed himself against the wall.

"Wow," Kara said, exhaling raggedly. "It's… Well, take a look."

They peered round the door. A figure stood just inside, staring back at them.

"It's a statue," Nate whispered.

A man's head and shoulders were carved from stone, lashed with rope to a marble plinth. He had a proud nose and blank white eyes beneath a curly mop of hair.

Kara edged past into the room beyond. It was large and unlit, the ceiling too high to make out. But in the glow from the stairway she could see a forest of stone figures stretching off into the gloom. There were other shapes too, vases and paintings and piles of crates stacked unevenly.

"I bet they're from a museum," Nate whispered as they crept through. "That's where they keep stuff from olden times. There's one in Frisco; my dad used to take me. They had pistols and a stagecoach; they even had this pod that some guys went to the moon in."

Kara laughed. "That's just a story."

"No, it really happened," Nate insisted. "It wasn't much bigger than the *Marlin*. And— Hey, look!"

Set into the wall ahead was a row of shutters, and a board printed with a single red word.

"News," Kara read. "I guess it means we go down there."

There was a narrow opening beside the news stand and a tunnel sloping down. Kara held up her hands as the light faded, drowning them in darkness. The thought of Singh following made her feel a little safer, but he'd be just as blind as they were.

"I think this used to be a train station," Nate whispered. "A stop on the underground network."

"I don't really know what those things are," Kara admitted.

"Trains were like buses," Nate said. "But big, hundreds of people could go in one. And stations were where they'd pick up passengers. There would've been thousands of folks coming down here every day."

Kara tried to picture these dark halls filled with light and people, all going places. The world must've been so different then.

Their footsteps echoed as they emerged into another open space. Kara stubbed her toe and cursed. "More statues," she complained, feeling her way. "Perfect."

"We should've brought a flashlight," Nate whispered. "Like they did. Look."

He was right – in the blackness up ahead Kara could see a beam of light glancing off the walls. Stilling her breath she heard voices too, distant and indistinct.

"Redeye," she hissed excitedly. "We're not too late."

"Too late for what?" a voice asked, and light blinded their eyes. "Put 'em up, both of you."

It was the narrow-faced Mariner, his pistol trained on them.

Nate raised his hands. "Kipps, it's me. Don't shoot."

The man smirked crookedly, then he raised his voice. "Hey, Redeye. I found your friends."

"Which ones?" Redeye called. "I have so many."

Kipps gestured with his torch. "The traitor and the mudfoot girl. I'm bringing them to you."

"Kara?" Redeye laughed. "I thought you'd be rotting in some MetCo cell."

"I didn't want to miss this," Kara shouted back.

Kipps directed them between the statues, his torch flashing across the faces of men and animals, making them shift and grimace. Redeye turned towards them as they stepped out into the open, his briefcase clutched in his hand. "I am genuinely happy to see you both," he said. "Kara because I love that you don't quit, however many times we try to kill you. And Nate because you know the sort of pointless trivia that might actually help right now."

"You want to know which of these statues is Wellington," Nate realised.

"Bravo," Redeye clapped. "Elroy died before he could explain what the notes on his map actually meant. The rest were obvious, but now we have six tunnels and one clue. So I need you to tell me which of these people, or horses, or whatever that thing is, are called Wellington."

Nate frowned. "What if I refuse?"

"He'll shoot me," Kara said. "And he'll probably torture you."

Redeye grinned. "Smart girl."

"Would you tell him?" Nate asked Kara. "If it was you?"

"Definitely," she said. "Then I'd find a way to hurt him later. He's not that bright, so it shouldn't be hard."

Redeye laughed, waving his gun at her. "Maybe I'll

shoot you right now, just for fun."

"It's that one," Nate said quickly, pointing at a massive iron sculpture of a man on a rearing horse. He held a sword, thrusting it towards the far left-hand tunnel. "I'm pretty sure. I mean, he looks like a Duke to me."

"He's right," Pavel grunted, turning his torch on the dusty floor. "It's been moved."

"Elroy's work," Redeye said. "It seems the boy knows his ancient historical junk after all. But now I have another problem. Obviously I can't let you go; you'd follow us and do something annoying. But believe it or not I've actually grown fond of you, Kara. I really don't want to kill you. Luckily I have a solution." He turned to the pinch-faced Mariner. "Kipps, wait until we're gone, then shoot them both. You can catch us up."

Kipps grinned toothily. "It's done."

"If it makes you feel any better," Redeye said as he backed towards the tunnel, "you'd never have survived what's coming. Cortez would've made sure of that."

He strode away into the darkness, Pavel on his heels. The light from their torches was soon swallowed up.

"Move." Kipps gestured with his pistol. "No, not in front of him. Get out of the way."

"No," Kara said, shielding Nate.

"But when I shoot you you'll fall down, then I'll shoot

him anyway. It's—"

There was a flash in the dark and the slam of a gunshot. Kipps hit the ground, his pistol tumbling from his hand.

"Shoot again," Kara called out. "In case they're listening."

"Oh, right." Singh emerged from the shadows, firing once into the air. Kara heard the crack of tiles.

"What took you so long?" she asked as he took the cuffs from his belt, yanking the groaning Mariner off the floor and chaining him to the wall. "You let Redeye get away."

"There were three of them," Singh pointed out. "I might've shot one, even two. The last one would've killed you. Now the odds are better."

Kipps's eyes fluttered as they moved towards the passageway. Blood soaked through his shirt and he strained against the cuffs. "You can't stop Cortez," he said. "If you try to fight him, he'll demolish your precious Shanties."

Kara turned back. "Not if we demolish him first."

22

The Back Door

Joe sat upright on a cold stone floor, his hands tied in front of him. They'd yanked the rag doll from his mouth but the oily taste of it was still foul on his tongue. He was in the basement of a tall tower, the levels above rotted out. Light came filtering down through clouds of dust and the floor was strewn with white objects in higgledy piles. Squinting, he realised it was bits of bathroom furniture – toilets and sinks and mirrored cabinets, all disconnected and discarded.

The ragged boy perched on the edge of a claw-footed bathtub, a spring-lock blade in one hand, Joe's bear in the other. He was whittling with his knife, carving off thin strips of plastic, sharpening Growly's legs into pointed stumps. His tongue protruded between his teeth as he worked.

"He lost one arm being kidnapped by Mariners," Joe said. "And the other when I got attacked by a shark."

The boy looked at him dubiously, then he lowered the bear. "Why you come here?" he asked. "Why, if you not Rubble King spy?"

"I was with some friends," Joe explained. "We were looking for a door."

The boy gave a nod of understanding. "I heard of folks like you. Trying to find the door, trying to go to the special place. Ain't been one since the last chief, but Doorkeepers always find them before they find it. We show them the way."

"You show them?" Joe asked. "So you know where the door is?"

"Course!" the boy said. He rose to his feet, pulling Joe up. In among the piles of porcelain a group of grey-faced Doorkeepers sat round a small fire, turning something on a spit. Joe saw pointed ears and scorched ginger fur. Beyond them was a circular archway like a tunnel's mouth, so deep in shadow he hadn't noticed it before. The ragged boy pointed. "The door."

The other children bowed their heads. "The door, the door," they murmured.

Joe crossed towards it, his eyes adjusting slowly. The tunnel was shallow, its end blocked with a huge circle of solid metal. He knew right away what he was looking at. The back door was three times his height and perfectly smooth, with no hinge or handle.

"How do you open it?"

The ragged boy came up behind him. "Open it?" he whispered. "Can't open it. Door stays shut until He comes."

"He?" Joe asked, touching the cool surface with his tied hands. "Who's He?"

"None knows," the boy said. "But he'll take us through to the special place, just like the others who came looking."

"So these others went through the door? They managed to open it?"

The boy shook his head, then confusingly he nodded. "They go through. But they not open the door."

Joe frowned. "So how did they go through?"

"The same way everyone else," the boy said, holding up the plastic bear. "They meet the Doorkeepers, and we send them on their way."

In a flash Joe realised what he meant. "No," he said. "You don't have to—"

The boy lashed out, Growly's sharpened legs cutting twin furrows in Joe's upper arm. Blood flowed – just a trickle, but enough to shock him out of his stupor. He ducked as the ragged boy lunged again, forcing him back against the hard steel door.

"Don't fear," the boy grinned, advancing. "We send you where you want to go."

There was a sudden clang and a high-pitched whine. Sparks flew as a bullet ricocheted from the door, slamming into the opposite wall. The children shrieked and Joe turned. Booted feet descended the steep concrete ramp that led back up into the light.

"Joe?" Maura called down. "I see you've been making friends."

Kara clutched Kipps's torch as they stepped into a long thin room with white walls and only half a floor. Peering over the edge she saw steel rails enveloped in decades of dust.

"This must be where the trains would come in," Nate whispered.

"The footprints go that way," Singh said, pointing. They climbed down on to the tracks.

In the tunnel the air was cool. Pipes and cables sprouted from the walls all criss-crossed with glistening webs. In the torchlight Kara saw a spider the size of her fist scuttling out of sight. Between the tracks the dust was so deep it was like walking on a thick carpet, if carpets sometimes rustled and squeaked when you trod on them.

The tracks sloped downward and she heard Nate shiver. "We must be under the old River Thames. They filled it in when the Wall went up, cleared the whole area. Which means..."

"We're under the Wall," Kara realised, looking up. "It can't be far now."

"You should put that light out," Singh said. "They could be watching."

Kara did as he said, tracing the rail with her foot. She could only imagine what she looked like shuffling along like a zombie, her peach dress smeared with filth. She wondered where Redeye was now – at the back door, or even through it? Had Cortez already arrived? Were his troops right now massing by the Wall, ready to swarm down this tunnel and murder everyone inside?

The thought of it made her pick up the pace, hurrying the others along. She was moving so fast that she slammed face first into a steel barrier that stood blocking the way.

She rubbed her nose. "Who put a wall there?"

"I think it's a train," Singh said. "It must've been down here forever."

Kara felt the obstruction with her hands. "There's a gap at the side. Nate, can you fit?"

"Of course," the boy said defensively, taking a deep breath.

They slid alongside the train, their backs to the wall. The air was thick with dust and the stink of oil and chemicals; Kara had to fight to stop herself sneezing. That's all we need, she thought. A city lost because I couldn't keep it in.

Then Singh stopped, drawing his pistol. "Look. The last carriage."

There was light up ahead, leaking through the open doors of the final train compartment. In the stillness Kara could hear voices.

"It's them," she whispered. "And see, there."

Ahead of the train the tracks stopped dead, hitting a wall of inward-curving metal. It filled the tunnel, a smooth circle of polished steel inset with a single blinking panel. The back door.

Kara crept closer, holding her breath. They'd almost reached the carriage when Pavel appeared in the doorway, looking at them in surprise. "Oh," he said. "It's you." And he raised his weapon.

Singh fired first, the roar of his pistol filling the tunnel. Pavel was thrown backwards off his feet, tumbling into the train carriage, blasting wildly as he fell. Singh staggered back, hitting the wall. Then he sank to the floor of the tunnel, blood coursing from his shattered left knee.

Kara dropped at his side, her hands trembling. It had

all been so sudden, and so loud.

"I'm OK," Singh said hoarsely. "Just need to sit for a minute."

There was a scuffling sound inside the train car, followed by a roar of bitter anger.

"Don't move," Kara called out shakily. "Stay there or we'll shoot you too."

"You killed him," Redeye said. "You didn't have to do that. Pavel was a good man."

"I'm sorry," Kara said, taking a step closer to the open doorway. "But we can't let you do this. We can't let you open the back door, and we can't let Cortez come through."

Redeye put his head out of the carriage, looking at her in complete bafflement. "Say again?"

"We won't let Cortez through," Kara repeated. "We won't let your men invade the City."

Redeye frowned, then he ducked back inside. "Let me get this straight. You think I'm trying to open this door so Cortez and his men can take over the City?" He laughed, a short, barking sound. "I know you think I'm stupid Kara, but that would have to be the dumbest plan of all time. How many troops do you think can fit on the *Kraken*? Eight, nine hundred? And how many do MetCo have guarding London? Five times that. Also, if that *was* the plan, why would I need this bomb?"

Kara stepped into the doorway, her heart seizing. Pavel lay sprawled on the linoleum floor, his arms flung wide. Beside him Redeye knelt over the briefcase, his sharp features lit by the glow of a computer panel. In the case Kara could see two vials of green liquid and a large red button.

"A bomb?" she asked, totally confused. "W-why?"

Redeye smiled thinly. "What's above our heads? I'll give you a clue, it's big and white and it keeps the sea out."

"You're insane," Singh said, struggling up. His face was pale and his trousers were soaked with blood. "It'd take an atomic weapon to bring down the Wall."

"Who says this isn't one?" Redeye asked. "OK, it isn't. But what if we don't want to bring it down? What if we just want to make a hole in it? Like pulling the plug of the world's biggest bathtub. Maximum mayhem, minimum property damage."

"So you are trying to take over," Kara said.

Redeye shrugged. "It's complicated."

"And what about the people in the City?" Nate asked. "What happens to them?"

"Some will die in the initial panic," Redeye admitted. "Some will drown when the waters rise high enough. And some will escape to the Shanties, where… Well, that'd be telling." He shook his head. "But let's be honest, they deserve whatever they get. Kara knows what I'm talking about, don't you? I saw the way you looked at them, back in the City. They disgust you too."

Kara wanted to deny it, but she couldn't. She remembered how sick she'd felt witnessing all that wealth and waste, while her own people suffered outside. Would she honestly care if it was all washed away? Then she remembered the other Kara, who'd helped her even though she didn't need to. She remembered the cabbie – what had he ever done? And she took a step closer.

"You can't escape," she said. "Just back away from the bomb and let's talk."

"You know I can't," Redeye said, raising his palm over the red button. "Cortez didn't lie: this really is a better world we're bringing. And besides, I don't want to."

He brought his hand down.

Singh fired but his pistol clicked empty.

Kara cried out, waiting for the explosion.

Redeye burst into laughter. "You should see your faces," he spluttered. "Honestly, Kara, I'm not suicidal. All I did was start the timer. You see? Now I have five minutes to get out of here."

Numbers ticked down on a digital readout. Redeye

jumped to his feet, stepping down from the train carriage and retreating along the tunnel. "I'm afraid I can't let you follow me this time," he said, waving his pistol. "Things are in motion, I can't have you messing them up."

He reached the back door, turning to the giant steel hatch and pressing his thumb down on the central panel. A light pulsed green, hydraulic pipes hissing as the door swung open.

"Goodbye, MetCo man," Redeye said. "And you, traitor. And farewell, Kara. You're truly one of the most remarkable people I've ever met. I'm sorry it has to end like this."

"But it doesn't have to," Kara pleaded. "You can still switch it off. You told me once that Mariners didn't kill unless they had to. You said you weren't monsters."

Redeye frowned thoughtfully. "Most Mariners aren't," he said. "But I think maybe I am."

And he ducked through the door into the dark.

Kara flung herself forward but the hatch was already closing, sealing with a resounding boom. Locks clicked into place and the panel went dead; she pressed her thumb on it but nothing happened. Who had told it to recognise Redeye's print? The friend, of course. He seemed to have access to every system in the City. But who had that kind of power? A suspicion was forming, but she couldn't bring herself to think it.

"It's no use," Nate said. "We have to leave."

"And go where?" Kara asked. "In four minutes this tunnel's going to explode."

"If we run we might make it," Nate insisted. "We might have a chance."

"And what about Singh?" Kara said in a low voice. "Are we supposed to carry him? We'll never—"

"Kara," Singh's voice echoed from inside the train carriage. "Come here, quickly."

He had dragged himself up, leaving a trail of blood. Now he was bent over the briefcase, the panel lighting his ashen face. "You won't believe this," he said, mopping the sweat from his brow, "but I think I can defuse it. Years ago I worked for the bomb squad; we used to train on devices just like this. I think I can make it stop."

Kara almost laughed. "But that's incredible."

Singh eased the rear panel off the bomb, revealing a nest of wires. "Sometimes you just get lucky. But listen, I can't focus with you two standing there. Nate's right, you should run."

"No," Kara said. "I won't leave you. It's not fair, you—"

"I'm not asking," Singh said.

"Kara." She felt Nate's hand in hers. "Come on. Please."

She turned, ready to protest. Then she saw his soot-streaked face, so serious and scared. If she died down here, so would he. And then Joe would be left alone.

"It's OK," Singh said, looking up. His mouth was tight with pain but his eyes were clear. "I'm right where I need to be. I should thank you, really. After all those years at MetCo, you've finally given me the chance to do something meaningful." He waved them away with one bloody hand. "Now go and save the world."

23

High Water

When the hatch began to open, the Doorkeepers fell to their knees, wailing in holy terror. Clouds of hydraulic gas gushed into the chamber and Joe shielded his eyes, backing away.

"He comes!" the ragged boy cried, dropping the toy bear. Redeye strode like a spectre from the steam, his long coat billowing around him, his electronic eye gleaming like a laser sight.

Then his gaze fell on Joe, and he blinked in surprise. "Joe? What are you doing here?"

There was a pistol shot and Redeye ducked, cursing and raising his weapon.

"I said you'd regret pulling a gun on me," Maura called out. "Now put that down and—"

Redeye fired back indiscriminately, peppering the

room with pellets. Sinks and toilet bowls exploded, the air filling with ceramic dust. The children scattered, Maura ducked, and Joe snatched Growly and turned to run. But Redeye had hold of his collar, yanking him back.

"Come out or I'll shoot the boy," he shouted. Then he laughed. "Would you believe I did almost this exact same dance with the other one, just a few moments ago?"

"You've seen Kara?" Joe asked. "She's alive?"

"Last I looked," Redeye said, shoving him towards the low wall where Maura was hiding, keeping his pistol pointed at Joe's head. "Listen, Shore ... woman. The clock is literally ticking, so get out here or I'll kill him. You know I don't mess around."

For a moment Joe thought she was going to stay put and seal his fate. But Maura rose resentfully to her feet, tossing her weapon aside. "You can't escape," she said. "My boys will be back any moment, and there are many more in the Pavilion waiting for your friend Cortez."

Redeye growled with frustration. "We *really* don't have time for this. OK, you're both coming with me. Cortez will want the boy, and you can be a bargaining chip if your people try anything."

He started up into the light, boots grinding on the concrete. But a plaintive voice called "W-wait," and Redeye turned. The ragged boy stood in a ring of shattered porcelain, his hands clasped beseechingly. "A-aren't you going to lead us to the special place?"

Redeye frowned. "What's he talking about?"

Joe looked back regretfully. Yes, the boy had wanted to eat him. But he couldn't feel bitter – this could've been him if things had gone differently. If he'd never met Kara.

"You came through the door," he explained. "They think you're a god."

Redeye snorted. "I'm flattered. But you've got the wrong guy."

And he hurried up into the daylight, the others following. They were almost at the boats when the world exploded.

Kara was shoving Nate up on to the station platform when the air was filled with blinding light, and the loudest noise either of them would ever hear. A wave of heat ripped through the tunnel, lifting them like leaves and slamming them against the wall. Kara's eyes burned and her ears rang but she managed to drag herself up, tugging at Nate's collar. She heard the rush of water behind them. The ocean was loose in the tunnel.

The cuffs were still hooked to the wall but Kipps had managed to pick them and escape; there was no sign of him now. Stone faces loomed from the shadows and

Kara could feel the air itself thrumming as water surged through the station, rattling the walls with the force of its approach. They sprinted past the silent news stand, the light from the doorway leading them on.

"Singh said he could stop it," Kara gasped as they slammed into the stairwell, heaving the door shut behind them. "He promised."

"He lied," Nate said, following her up. "You knew that, right? He didn't want to slow us down."

Kara felt her mind roll over. Yes, perhaps a part of her had known. And now a good man was gone.

There was a terrible groan, and looking over the handrail she saw the door tearing from its hinges and tumbling into the dark. A jet of water shot through the opening, the walls buckling on either side. The water roared like an animal, swirling and smashing and swallowing up the stairwell as they ran. Light bulbs popped one by one.

Then they were at the top, tumbling into the passage where the guards lay lifeless. Kara heard shouts in the distance, but they saw no one as they climbed stone steps to an echoing entrance hall lined with gloomy paintings. The walls shuddered violently, arched windows raining showers of coloured glass. A silver suit of armour toppled from its plinth, the sword tip snagging Nate's shirt as the whole thing clattered in pieces on the flagstone floor.

They emerged into a gravel courtyard dotted with trees. In the far fence a gate stood open and they sprinted towards it. To the left a concrete yard was jammed with black vehicles, desperate figures fleeing the building and piling into them. A van had flipped in the entranceway and a gaggle of smartly dressed people stood arguing over the best way to move it. Kara saw a face she recognised – the minister from the Pavilion screaming at a cowering subordinate. *It won't do any good,* Kara thought. *They were powerful before, now they're as helpless as anyone else.*

But as they reached the fence she realised she hadn't seen anyone in MetCo blue; even the sentries had fled. She remembered the chaos in the corridor, the empty offices and the truck loaded with equipment. Almost as if they'd known what was coming.

The tremors subsided, and suddenly all was still. Kara turned in the gateway, taking a long, ragged breath. The Houses of Parliament stood over them, a square-sided mountain of stone in the shadow of the Wall. Were they panicking for nothing? Maybe the water had been dammed somehow; the basement might've fallen in or the tunnel itself could have collapsed. Surely no force on Earth could bring down a building so proud and ancient and strong?

Then she saw trickles of black water leaking from the

windows. With a pop one of them burst, then another, water gushing out in strengthening floods. All along the ground floor glass began to shatter, jets shooting out like riot cannons. A door ripped from its hinges, cartwheeling into the courtyard on a rolling black tide. Nate grabbed Kara and they ran.

Beyond the fence was a grassy square, groups of onlookers staring in disbelief at the torrent of water flowing from the building. "Which way?" Nate asked.

Kara shook her head. "I came a really long way round."

He pulled out his tablet. "Joe's 'x' is here, and that's south. The tunnel's to the west, so it should be up that way."

"I thought you failed navigation?"

Nate shrugged. "If I'm wrong, you won't be mad for long."

They'd reached the far side of the square when they heard an awful rending creak. Parliament had become a waterfall, black torrents cascading from the windows on the second and third storeys. The clock tower began to list, leaning away from the shuddering building like the mast of a storm-driven ship. The bells of Big Bill chimed madly as the tower fell, striking the Wall and shattering into a thousand fragments of metal and masonry.

And with that, the Houses of Parliament seemed to give

up. The building toppled in on itself, walls crumbling and roofs caving as the internal structure collapsed. There was a deep unearthly groan, then the entire edifice exploded outwards, chunks of stone borne up on a geyser of white water. A rock the size of a bus landed nearby, gouging a crater in the ground. Kara saw people scattering and others who weren't fast enough. Rain began to fall, thick with glass and dust. Parliament was gone. In its place stood a fountain, punching at the sky.

Again they ran, into a long street lined with grand stone residences. Tarmac cracked and trees crashed down, one huge trunk flattening three parked cars. Doors flew open, terrified people hauling sacks and boxes filled with possessions. Roof tiles fell like a rain of blades.

They came to a park, joining a knot of people all fleeing in the same direction. A toddler wailed, gazing over his mother's shoulder at the geyser in the distance. A man shoved past wearing white underpants and carrying a tiny dog; he cursed as it snapped at his face. On a nearby lake white birds drifted serenely, unaware of the spreading panic.

Scaling a set of marble steps they found themselves facing a fenced building even more impressive than the one they'd just escaped from. Flags fluttered from the roof and the courtyard teemed with people in gowns and robes, all bustling around an elderly man who hobbled on a golden cane. "That's the king!" Nate managed between breaths. "I've seen him in clips."

The old man climbed into a cage made of metal and glass; Kara had never seen anything like it. On the roof a pair of crossed blades began to rotate, thrumming noisily as they picked up speed. Then with a rush of air the whole thing lifted off the ground, gleaming like a black steel insect.

"A copter," Nate said in astonishment as the machine lifted above the palace, angling towards the Wall. "I never saw one in real life."

They came to a sloping park, people pressing in around them as they ran a weeping woman, a boy Kara's age, a young man with blood streaming down his forehead. Then they broke through a line of trees and found themselves facing the dark mouth of the Gullet. Kara felt her hopes sink.

Thousands of people had already reached the cobbled plaza, shoving towards the tunnel. The roads were jammed, cars and buses grinding to a halt as the panic spread. And still more people were rushing in, darting between the cars, slamming into the crowds that were forcing their way slowly, painfully towards the Gullet.

"Whatever happens," Kara said. "Hold on to me."

Nate gulped and nodded.

Fights broke out; she heard people yelling, punches being thrown. More than once they were slammed aside by someone big and determined, forging through the crowd like a boat through chop. Kara squeezed Nate's hand, feeling the world spin. The courage she'd felt before had been driven from her; now she was drowning in cold fear. She tried to fight it down, to steady herself. Panicking would achieve nothing; they were in enough trouble already. She gulped air, trying not to scream. The crowd surged around them.

"We need more power," Redeye growled as the engine protested noisily. But the tide was too strong, dragging the speedboat backwards. Rubble shifted and slid and the air rang with the clatter of stones. Joe crouched on the bench seat, seeing towers tumble as their foundations were torn out by the whirlpool forming at the base of the Wall.

Hearing a shout, he turned. From the hollow beneath the tall tower small grey figures came tumbling, bounding over the rocks and splashing into the water, leaping from one rubble heap to the next as the ground shook. Water swelled behind them, a great wave bubbling from the depths.

But on its crest Joe saw something small and white

riding the current. Hands gripped the sides of the claw-footed bathtub, the ragged boy and the pale girl clinging on as the tide drove them forward. She raised a hand and Joe waved back, watching as their makeshift craft tossed and twisted, borne away into the labyrinth of stone.

Then the tower began to topple, chunks of concrete splashing into the water all around them. Redeye gave a yell as one of them slammed into the instrument panel. Sparks flew and the engine died. Joe squeezed his eyes shut as they were dragged back, the current pulling them down.

Then suddenly the roaring stopped. The boat tipped forward as waves crashed against the Wall, then sluiced back towards them. Maura looked around in astonishment. "What's happening?"

"Something's blocked the tunnel," Redeye said. "But it won't hold for long."

He bent over the broken panel, reaching inside. There was a flash and he pulled back, cursing.

Maura lifted her head, peering through the clouds of dust for any sign of her Shore Boys. After the initial explosion they'd heard distant shouts and gunfire in the gloom, but that was minutes ago at least. Joe couldn't stop thinking about Kara – how close had she been to that terrible blast?

"You did this," he said, turning on Redeye. "Didn't you? You did it, and now Zuma's dead, and those kids, and … and…" He couldn't bring himself to say it.

Redeye yanked out a pair of wires. "None of them should've been out here. It's their own fault."

Joe snarled. He wanted to hit Redeye, to spit in his good eye, but he knew it wouldn't make any difference. "It must be horrible being you," he said. "You don't care about anything or anyone."

Redeye looked up. "It's like I told Kara. I care so much I'm willing to kill for it." He returned to his task, twisting the wires together. "You asked me once how I got the eye. I'll tell you if you like."

The air was motionless, like it was waiting for something. Joe heard a distant creak like shifting pack ice. "OK," he said.

"I was about your age," Redeye began, sparks lighting his face. "My mother was a scavenger but we scraped by. We lived near a city called New Orleans, where the Mariners were regular visitors. Mom traded with them; she liked them, and they liked her. They said, come west. Bring your boy. We have a city where you'll be safe. So she bought an old desert buggy and a few tanks of chem fuel and we set out."

He turned the key and the engine fired, nudging the

boat forward. Redeye shifted gears, steering between the shattered towers. "We were deep in the desert when the bandits came. They killed my mother, then they took me to this place, a bunker with a steel dish outside. The scientists who lived there gave them food and medicines, and in return they got me.

"At first the scientists just kept me in a cage. They fed me, asked me a lot of questions, it wasn't so bad. Then after a few months they said they had something special planned. An operation that would make me unique in all the world. When they put me to sleep I was actually excited."

A building crumbled close by, concrete sliding into the sea, but Redeye barely paused, his knuckles white on the wheel. He wasn't just telling the story, Joe realised. He was reliving it.

"I woke up with this pain in my head like a hot needle. Something had gone wrong, they told me. The experiment hadn't worked. The electronic eye was supposed to fuse with my brain stem, allow me to see over distances, track heat signatures, all that stuff. But all it did was hurt constantly."

"But you got away?" Joe asked.

Redeye shook his head. "They ditched me. All I did was eat and cry so they left me in the desert. But I was tougher than they knew. I survived. I headed west. I met Elroy. I made it out."

"Did you know…?" Joe started. "Before you set off that bomb today, did you know kids would die? That their mums would die, just like what happened to you?"

Redeye's head lifted. The gears in his eye socket ground softly, the glow shifting. "It needed to happen, Joe. For a better world to come."

"I bet that's what those scientists thought too."

"Don't compare me to them," Redeye snarled. "They tortured me. They—"

"You're worse," Joe said softly. "I think you're worse."

A new sound was building now, an abyssal groan like the Earth itself was shifting somewhere deep beneath them. Redeye slammed the throttle and the speedboat ploughed forward, the petrol engine growling. The water surged again, driving against the hull.

Maura's grip tightened suddenly on Joe's arm. "I don't believe it," she said, almost a whisper.

Redeye glanced back, and his mouth dropped. "OK, I may have used a little too much explosive," he shouted, before his words were drowned out by a howl like a dying planet.

Dust billowed into the air. Through it Joe could see tons of concrete, sliding and subsiding into the churning white water. It was impossible, but it was happening. The Wall was falling.

In the mouth of the Gullet, the crowd screamed with a single voice. Across the park and the distant rooftops Kara could see right through to the Wall. The sight of it made her heart stop.

A massive stretch of concrete had begun to slump, like a great back breaking as the Earth opened beneath it. It toppled forward, crushing the buildings below. Into the gap the ocean roared, ripping and grinding as it thundered through the breach.

The wave drowned everything in its path, tearing the roofs from houses, wrenching trees from their roots. Kara saw the palace go under, the grey tide slamming through the iron fence and swallowing the building whole. And still it kept coming, washing up the green slope and crashing against a wall of towers below the park.

This at least seemed to hinder the wave's path. It broke at last, spilling forth a torrent of black filth that rolled inexorably towards them. The crowd broke too, shoving towards the tunnel in a wild, desperate mob. Kara clung to Nate's hand as they were driven onwards, crushed in a fleshy vice.

She saw a skinny boy vaulting on top of the crowd,

springing from head to head like stepping stones. She saw an old man standing over a toppled cart, spilling jewellery and paintings, shouting furiously as they were trampled into the dirt. She saw a pregnant woman, her arms wrapped round her belly, gritting her teeth and snarling at anyone who got too close. She saw a MetCo officer weeping, tearing the badge from his chest. As they entered the tunnel she felt soft shapes beneath her feet, and didn't dare look down.

The cries of the crowd took on a deep, echoing note as they passed into the Gullet. The lights flickered and Kara felt her chest tighten. *Please*, she thought. *If anyone's listening, God or whoever. Don't let me die in the dark with all these people.*

She heard splashing and felt cold water around her feet. The tide had caught them, washing through the park. The shrieks grew louder, the crowd clambering over the security barriers in grasping floods. Now the water was up to Kara's ankles, now her shins. She tried to steady herself and keep moving.

Past the barrier, the tunnel sloped upward. They left the water behind, marching on dry concrete, the bulbs in the ceiling casting a cold yellow light. On they went, deeper and deeper, and Kara tried not to listen to the howls behind them as the water rose, tried not to think about what must be happening back there in the City.

Then suddenly the crowd stopped, wedged in the narrowing tunnel, unable to move. Kara felt the water again, creeping up her legs. The lights flickered out and there was a roar of terror.

24

Democracy

The speedboat angled through the water, leaving the Badlands and entering the Southern Cut. Behind them the sun was just starting to sink, though to Joe it felt like days since they'd set out. Redeye eased back and the boat idled, gliding between steep-sided tankers. Men stood at the railings high above, gawping as black smoke rose on the horizon.

"What now?" Joe asked. He still didn't fully understand what was happening – the Wall was broken and the City was flooded, but there was no sign of the *Kraken*. Which meant there was more to come; Cortez's plan was still in motion.

"Now we come to the interesting part," Redeye said, taking out his macrobinoculars and angling them towards the Pavilion. He passed them over and Joe peered through.

The scene was one of utter chaos.

Bedraggled city folk were spilling from the Gullet, filling the concrete square. Some had children on their backs; others were wounded and had to be helped or carried. Joe looked for Kara, but there were too many people – thousands of grim faces in the dying light. *She must have made it*, he thought. *She's the smartest, toughest person I know. Please, I can't face it out here on my own.*

The Zoo had emptied too, a wall of blue uniforms marching down the steps to form a holding line round the swelling crowd of city refugees. This seemed strange to Joe – shouldn't MetCo be leading people out into the Shanties, to make room for more? Others clearly thought the same – he saw a suited city man arguing with an officer on the steps. The man gestured angrily towards the Shanties, but the cop drew her pistol and the man stepped back.

"What a mess you've made," Maura told Redeye, taking the binoculars from Joe and squinting through. "And for what?"

"For this," Redeye said, grinning. "By nightfall Cortez will own your precious Shanties."

Maura snorted. "My Shore Boys are going to have something to say about that. And so will he."

A familiar figure came striding from the Zoo, his head

raised defiantly. Remick was flanked by riot troops as he stopped at the top of the steps, pulling a transmitter from his pocket.

"Citizens, remain calm," he said, his voice echoing from the speakers. "MetCo are in control. I promise, very soon we'll know exactly who was behind this."

"Does your captain really think he can take on the Shore Boys and MetCo together?" Maura sneered. "It'll be a slaughter."

Redeye shook his head. "I can't believe you still haven't figured it out. Think. How did three Mariners get inside the City carrying a bomb, and who coded my thumbprint into the back door? Who got Elroy into the tunnels for his recon mission, and who's allowing the *Kraken* to pass through the security cordon unhindered? There's only one man who could make all that happen."

Maura's face dropped. "H-he couldn't," she gasped. "We had an agreement. I've been paying him for years."

"And he's been planning this for longer," Redeye said. "Ever since our patrol ships picked him up. I've heard the story from Cortez so many times. He was sent to interrogate Remick, but it didn't take them long to realise how much they had in common. Remick was Shanty-born – he hates the City every bit as much as we do."

"So he betrayed his own people?" Joe asked. "He's

going to let Cortez invade the Shanties?"

"You don't understand," Redeye said. "We're not here to conquer; we're here to collaborate. No harm will come to anyone in the Shanties, not unless they start trouble. This will become the Mariners' new European hub; there'll be no more poverty, no more hunger. No more gangs either. Your Shore Boys will have to find a new line of work. Luckily there'll be plenty to go round."

Maura looked away, disgusted. "And Cortez gets to treat us like his own personal fiefdom."

"Pot, meet kettle," Redeye snorted. "You've lorded over this place for years, getting rich while others starved. It's time for someone else to have a turn."

A sound broke in, so loud it was like a drill driving into Joe's head. He clamped his hands over his ears as the speakers screeched, feedback echoing from the face of the Wall. All across the Pavilion he saw others doing the same, covering their ears and wincing.

It stopped, and for a long moment there was silence. The Pavilion held its breath.

Then a new voice came through the speakers, loud and clear.

"People of London," it said. "Welcome to a new world!"

Kara had almost reached the steps when the noise came. She covered her ears, tugging Nate forward, using the distraction to dodge through the MetCo cordon and up towards the Zoo.

They'd fled from the tunnel moments before, shoving through the crowd of refugees hemmed in by MetCo's riot shields. *Why are they keeping them here?* Kara wondered. She had a horrible feeling she already knew.

Climbing the steps she could see across the Pavilion to the towers beyond. The people of the Shanties had been driven back but they hadn't gone far, jostling for space along the sea wall and in the windows of tall buildings. Kara saw Shore Boys in the crowd and wanted to go to them, find Maura and Joe, figure out what was happening. But there was someone she had to speak to first.

Then the voice spoke, and her blood froze.

"People of London!"

Nate shot upright. Kara grabbed his arm.

"Welcome to a new world!"

There was a rushing, rolling sound out in the Cut. The water began to churn, waves crashing against the shoreline towers. All across the Pavilion, heads began to turn.

The *Kraken*'s conning tower rose from the depths, the steel pillar barbed with black weaponry. Then the body surfaced, water streaming from the vast central cylinder. The crowds drew back as that scrawled and terrifying face was revealed, painted teeth fiercely bared.

The sub drifted forward, coming to rest against the harbour wall. Steel hatches sprang open along the entire length and soldiers spilled out, taking up positions along the flat-topped hull. Then a door flew open on the conning tower and Cortez strode on to the balcony, slender and upright in a coat of black oilskin. He faced the Pavilion, the Mariner symbol gleaming on his chest, his webbed hands grasping the railing. Behind him another figure lurked in the doorway. Dark hair and dark eyes – Cane.

Cortez scanned the crowd, raising a transmitter. "Greetings," he said, his voice echoing from the Wall and the concrete towers. "We are the Mariners, and we have come to set you free. Some of you, at least."

The refugees huddled closer, murmuring fearfully. Over in the Shanties Kara saw numberless faces, silently watching.

"First I'd like to address the displaced people from inside the Wall," Cortez began, "standing out here on this cold Pavilion. I offer apologies for all you've been through, whether you've lost your loved ones, or your homes, or your jewellery.

"But how long did you think you could get away with

269

it? How long did you think you could take, and take, and never give back? You let sick people die, knowing you could heal them. You let children starve, knowing you could feed them. If someone did that to my daughter –" he gestured to Cane – "I'd have their head. Think about that while I speak to the people I'm really concerned with."

He tilted his head, looking now at the crowds gathered along the sea wall and among the towers across the Cut. They crowded into every doorway, on to every roof and window ledge.

"Citizens of the Shanties," he said. "I know you've been told a pack of lies about my people. You think we're terrorists coming to murder you in your beds. *They* told you those stories." He pointed to the Pavilion. "The ministers and the media barons. They wanted you to feel powerless, trusting them to keep you safe.

"But the truth is we aren't so very different from you. We want the same things: peace, freedom, regular meals. But we don't hurt people to get it. We don't allow the powerful to exploit the weak." He lowered his voice conspiratorially, the crowd hanging on every syllable. "There's a word we Mariners hold dear. Those ministers do too. It's a powerful word, but it can be twisted out of all recognition. The word is 'democracy'.

"Britain is a democracy, they'll tell you. Every citizen has the right to vote. But how many Shanty folk have citizenship? Most of you are unregistered; you're immigrants or the children of immigrants. They know that. In fact, they depend on it. There are many more of you than there are of them."

He gripped the railing. "So I've come here today to give you back the rights you've been denied, starting with the right to vote. But there's only one issue on the table here. Life. Or death."

He waved a hand and the Mariners on the *Kraken* raised their rifles, pointing them out into the Pavilion. Kara heard screams, saw the refugees from the City trying to retreat, but there was nowhere for them to go.

"These people have exploited you since the day you were born," Cortez shouted over the din. "They've stolen your dignity. I believe that for these crimes they deserve to die. But I'm not a madman. I know there are children in this crowd; they should not suffer for the sins of their parents."

He tilted his head, looking up towards the Zoo. For a moment Kara was sure he'd seen her, but his gaze was fixed on Remick. "My old comrade, I believe the next part is up to you."

Kara looked at Nate, biting her lip as her worst fears

were confirmed. Shouts of betrayal echoed across the Pavilion but Remick ignored them, raising his transmitter. "Execute special order one-zero-one," he barked. "Take the children. Leave the rest."

Anarchy erupted. The MetCo line broke as officers stormed into the crowd, their batons raised. Kara saw babies snatched from their mothers' arms, boys younger than Joe dragged off their feet. Remick's men worked methodically, passing the children from one to another, hurrying them towards the steps and up into the Zoo.

Not every MetCo officer was part of it, Kara saw – by the docks a group of them stormed at their colleagues, fists and cudgels flying. They were joined by a handful of Shore Boys, trying their best to smash through the MetCo line. But it wouldn't be enough. She had to act.

Steeling herself, Kara lunged towards Remick. "Traitor!" she shouted, struggling as his men held her back.

Remick turned, smiling cruelly. "The Shanty girl," he said. "I hoped you'd drowned in one of our cells, but it seems Singh disobeyed my orders after all. Where is he?"

"Gone," Kara said. "He was trying to defuse Redeye's bomb."

"And he failed." Remick sighed. "The man was always weak."

"He was stronger than you'll ever be," Kara hissed. "He'd never betray his own people."

Remick sneered. "Who, them?" He jerked his chin towards the Pavilion. "They're not my people. They thought they could push me around because they had money and power, but they're nothing. You are my people, child. The Shanties are my people. And in our new world my people will want for nothing. The Mariners will bring jobs, money, trade. This place will be transformed."

Kara glanced towards Cortez; he stood on the balcony in discussion with one of his officers, ignoring the pandemonium below. "I don't believe you'd do all this just to hand everything over to the Mariners," she said. "What's in it for you?"

Remick smiled impishly, turning to gaze at the Wall looming over them. "What's in it for me? Only the greatest city in the world. A little waterlogged, perhaps, but our construction crews will soon fix that. King Remick, it has a nice ring, don't you think?"

"You're insane." Kara jerked forward, breaking free of the hands holding her. She swiped at Remick with one hand, slipping the other into his pocket before he could pull away. Then the guards seized her again, kicking her legs and shoving her down.

Nate knelt at her side. "Be careful. They'll shoot you if

you try that again."

Kara grinned. "It's OK. I got what I needed."

The doors to the Zoo slid shut, the children sealed inside. "It's done," Remick announced and Cortez looked up.

"Good. Then we can begin." He gripped the railing. "Now, it's perfectly simple. Those who believe these City people deserve a second chance, raise your hands. Those who know they deserve to die, do nothing. We'll take a—"

"I want to say something." Kara's voice leapt from the speakers, startling her. Her hands shook where she clutched the transmitter she'd snatched from Remick's pocket.

Cortez squinted, touching the scar on his cheek. "Is that … Kara? Neptune's beard, back from the dead. Remick, seize her."

"No!" Kara shouted as the guards lunged forward. Nate shoved them back, ignoring the guns in his face. "Let me speak. In a democracy you get to hear both sides, don't you?"

There was a rumble from the Shanties and Cortez's eyes narrowed. Then he nodded briskly. "Very well. Speak your piece. But keep it brief."

"I just…" Kara began, realising she had no idea what she was going to say. "I just wanted…" She had to appear strong, even if her insides were quivering and her knees were ready to collapse. She'd watched Remick and she'd watched Cortez; she'd seen the way they used words to persuade people, to win their trust. It was all about confidence and certainty.

"I just wanted to say, almost everything Cortez said is true," she started. "I grew up in the Shanties, just over there actually. And I love my home; it's big and it's crazy and it's full of all kinds of people. But I hate it too. There's hunger and disease, and danger everywhere you look. Most of us wake up each morning not knowing if we're going to eat, if we're going to work, or if we're going to be stabbed in an alley and dumped in the sea." A murmur of assent rose from the towers.

"And these people –" she gestured at the City refugees – "do nothing to help. They know it's tough out here, but I guess they just choose not to think about it."

She leant forward, knowing she had their attention. "I lost a good friend today. He died trying to stop all this from happening. He was a MetCo officer, just like Mr Remick. But he was brave and he was honest. Another friend helped us; he's right here." She indicated Nate, who blushed to his collar. "He's a Mariner, but he risked his life to stop Cortez because he doesn't think killing people is the right way to achieve anything."

"That boy's no Mariner," Cortez cut in. "He's a traitor to his people."

"Let me finish!" Kara snapped, her words reverberating in the silence. "I'm not speaking to you. I'm speaking to them. My people, not yours. I know you think you know us, but you don't. I know you think we'll look the other way but we're better than that."

She took a breath, mustering her strength. "I've lived in the Shanties, and I've sailed with the Mariners, and I've been inside the Wall. And this is what I've seen. There are bad people everywhere you go. Crooks and killers who don't care if you live or die as long as they come out on top. Powerful people who think they can twist you into doing whatever they want. But there are decent people too. People who help each other, who try to do the right thing, and sometimes they fail, and sometimes they don't."

She barely knew where the words were coming from any more; she was just letting them flow out of her, feeling more certain than she ever had in her life. "Cortez is right. Things have to change. But if we do it his way, if we turn our heads and let him kill all these people, we'll never forgive ourselves. We can find another way. We can make a better world, all of us, together. Please, let's try."

25

Broken Glass

Kara's voice died away and an unearthly stillness fell. Joe felt the tears come, blurring his view through the binoculars. He wanted to cry out, to tell her how proud he was, but she was so far away. Redeye watched silently, and Joe saw conflicting emotions pass across his face – frustration, yes, and bitterness. But was that admiration too?

Then a spark flared and Joe glanced down. On the boat's instrument panel the wires were still exposed. An idea began to form and he leant close to Maura. "Get ready," he whispered, and she nodded.

Cortez's voice echoed over the still water. "Now we've heard both sides. I'll admit, Kara makes an emotional case. But she's a child; she doesn't understand how the world works. If you let these people live, things will be back how they were within a year. Maybe there'll be a few different people in charge, a few more schools or hospitals to assuage their guilt. But nothing will have changed. And still the waters keep rising. How long can it go on?

"It's time to make a choice. If you agree with Kara, raise your hand. If you want to make a real future for the Shanties, remain as you are."

Joe held his breath, squinting through the binoculars. No hands were going up. The City refugees huddled together, waiting for the verdict. The people of the Shanties watched from roofs and window ledges, and to his dismay Joe saw some of them peeling away, dropping out of sight, running from the responsibility.

Then a voice called out and he saw a hand thrust skywards, above a tangle of red hair. "Kara!" Miss Ella shouted. "I'm with you!"

"Also me!" A young man reached up, sunlight gleaming on his black quiff.

A group of ANTI activists joined him, fists raised in a firm salute. Then a gang of Shanty kids followed their lead, grinning at each other. All along the edge of the Pavilion Joe saw scattered hands raised, people looking guardedly at their neighbours before reaching into the air.

Then the dam broke, rippling across the towers like

a wave. Hand after hand was thrust upward, a domino effect passing from block to block, from roof to roof, from ship to ship. Joe saw one man balanced on a crane above the harbour, sticking his hand up so fervently that he lost his balance and toppled a hundred feet into the water. He came up grinning, and shoved his hand in the air again.

Kara stood firm, her eyes fixed on Cortez. For a long time there was silence, then the Mariner captain shook his head. "I should've killed you when I had the chance."

"You made the rules," Kara replied. "Now take your submarine and leave."

Joe saw Cane behind her father, reaching to place a hand on his shoulder.

He shook her off. "No," he said. "Democracy be damned. Weapons, fire at will."

Below him on the *Kraken* the rocket banks spun into position, energy cannons humming as they took aim at the Pavilion. "Better move," Redeye said and turned the key, the motor rattling into life. Joe took a breath, slipping Growly from his pocket. The bear's legs jutted out like sharpened fangs. He winked at Maura and she nodded, backing up against the gunwale.

Brandishing his bear Joe leapt forward, jamming Growly legs-first into the instrument panel. Sparks flew, wires sheared and Redeye jerked back in surprise. Joe had been hoping the engine would sputter out, leaving them dead in the water. But instead the speedboat roared into high gear, shooting forward like a rocket. Maura was thrown over the side, her cry cut off as she hit the water. Redeye started up, drawing his pistol, but then a tanker hove into view and he was forced to grab the wheel.

Joe slid to the railing but before he could jump Redeye seized his ankle, yanking him back. "No, you don't."

Screams rose from the Pavilion and Joe saw missiles streaking into the sky, pillars of fire erupting. Black smoke billowed, lit by the golden sun. The noise was deafening.

Then for a moment he heard voices on the breeze, a chorus of them, crying the same word over and over. He felt his stomach roll over. Maybe there was hope after all.

When the firing started Kara's first thought was of Joe.

Nate pulled her down as flame-tailed rockets ripped the air and blue firebolts screamed from the *Kraken*'s rapidly spinning energy cannons. Gangplanks clattered from the submarine's landward side and the Mariners stormed into the harbour, firing as they came. The Pavilion was a surging mass of desperate panic; Kara could only imagine how many would be crushed in that terrible stampede. Then the missiles struck and the crowds vanished, swallowed by the black smoke.

"This is your fault!" Remick bellowed, storming towards her. "If you hadn't spoken up…"

"My fault?" she shouted back. "You trusted a terrorist and now everyone here is going to die."

A missile struck the face of the Zoo, the glass panes shattering outwards. Kara dropped, shielding herself from the storm of shards. When she raised her head Remick was lying on the concrete, his guards scattered around him.

"That was too close," Nate said, picking himself up. "We should get inside where it's safe." He gestured to the Zoo, now just a ragged steel hole in the face of the Wall.

"Not without him," Kara said, tugging Remick's arm. "He needs to pay for what he's done."

But Remick didn't move. Kneeling, Kara rolled him on to his back, his blood-stained wig flapping free. An inch-thick shard of glass was embedded in his neck, his face stricken in a hideous grimace. Explosions flared, reflected in his blank, lifeless eyes. One of the guards staggered to his boss's side, took one look and stumbled away, fleeing into the smoke.

Kara shut her eyes, struggling to breathe. It was all too much, all this death, all this noise. The world had gone mad, and she was trapped in the middle of it.

Then for the briefest second the rockets ceased and she heard raised voices carried on the breeze. It was a rallying cry, distant but unmistakable.

"Are they…?" Nate asked in amazement. "Are they shouting your name?"

"No," Kara said, hugging the ground as her head spun. "That's not… No."

"They are," Nate insisted. "They're shouting 'Kara, Kara'."

She turned away, towards the Zoo. The urge to hide was almost overwhelming; she wanted to run inside, find a dark place and never come out. But that was impossible now.

"I didn't … I didn't say those things so people would…" She gritted her teeth, gathering her strength. "I have to go down there. If they're fighting, I have to help them."

"You don't," Nate insisted. "Your speech was great but it doesn't make you responsible for everything that happens after."

"I think it does," Kara said. Then she took his hand. "Run if you want. Go to the Zoo, find those kids that Remick stole and keep them safe. I won't blame you. But I don't think I can."

Nate stared back at her, his clothes smeared with soot

and blood. "Don't be crazy. We're in this together. I mean, we'll almost certainly die a horrible death, but that's just the way it—"

There was an ear-shattering whine, echoing hoarsely as the damaged speakers crackled into life. The din of firing ebbed as a disembodied voice wheezed from the smoke.

"Kara," it said. "Kara, are you there?"

She lifted her head. Gunfire rattled in the dark.

"Perhaps you're dead already," Cortez continued, "but I've made that mistake before. I just want you to know that I have something of yours. If you come to the *Kraken*, unarmed and alone, I'll hand it over. And if you don't believe me, listen."

The speakers hissed and for a moment there was silence. Then a plaintive voice spoke, weak and frightened and very far away. "K-Kara?" Joe stuttered. "I'm so sorry. I'm so sorry."

26
Resistance

Cortez took the transmitter from Joe's hand, looking out across the *Kraken*'s railing to the wall of fire in the Pavilion. "Good," he said. "She'll come."

"She'll come," Joe said, trying to keep his voice steady, "and when she gets here, she'll kill you."

They'd arrived only moments before; Redeye had hauled Joe out of the speedboat and driven him along the sea wall towards the sub, soldiers saluting as they passed. They'd climbed the gangplank into a maze of steel corridors, following a winding stairway to find Cortez waiting on the balcony.

In the harbour Joe could see the shapes of dockside warehouses, most of them just heaps of rubble. Cries echoed in the gloom and there was a constant clatter of gunfire.

He clutched Growly; the bear's legs had melted into one twisted lump, but his fierce face still made Joe feel braver.

"There's been scattered resistance," Cortez was telling Redeye. "Some of the mudfoots are armed, but they can't hold out for long."

"Maura Glass and her Shore Boys," Redeye growled. "I should have gone back; we could've used her. Instead she's out there, making trouble."

"I could talk to her for you if you like," Joe offered, gesturing at the transmitter. "Maura would listen to me. We could stop all this. More people don't have to die for no reason."

Cortez turned on him. His blue eyes were laced with red.

"No reason?" he spat. "I gave them my reasons and they didn't listen. I even gave them a vote; I didn't have to do that."

"But they voted, and now you're killing them anyway."

Cortez looked away. "I'll do whatever it takes to bring a better world."

A grenade detonated close by, the red light dancing on his mask-like face. Looking down, Joe saw Mariner soldiers taking up positions around the sub, their weapons pointed outwards.

"What's happening down there?" Cortez demanded, his voice tightening. "What are they doing?"

Cane stepped on to the balcony, saluting nervously. Her face was smeared with oil, her lip quivering. "Father, I mean, C-Captain, the men are... You have to..."

"Say it," Cortez snapped.

"There are reports from the P-Pavilion," Cane stammered. "We're encountering more mudfoots than expected. They say the Shanty rats and the city scum are fighting together. And they're all armed – apparently these Shore Boys have been giving out guns."

Cortez cursed. "Where are MetCo? Where's that traitor Remick?"

"They're saying he's dead. Some of his men turned against us. The rest ran away."

"Cowards!" Cortez exclaimed. "Mudfoot cowards."

There was a high-pitched screech and a voice cried, "Incoming!"

A rocket struck the *Kraken*'s prow with a blinding flash, sending up a column of steam. Cortez was thrown off his feet, slamming back against the conning tower. Cane dropped at his side but he shoved her away, staggering up.

"Redeye, get down there and take charge. Drive the mudfoots back. Kill as many as you can. And if Kara comes, bring her to me."

Redeye nodded grimly. "It's done."

Kara and Nate crossed the Pavilion, wandering through a scene from hell. The concrete was patterned with scorch marks and blast craters, though there were fewer bodies than she'd expected – most of the refugees must have managed to flee into the Shanties.

Nate dropped beside a Mariner boy not much older than himself, spreadeagled on his back with a pistol in his hand. "I know him. He was on the *Neptune*. He punched me once because I trod on his foot."

Kara wondered what Cortez had said to the boy, what words he'd used to convince him to do this. "We have to stop him," she said. "Cortez needs to die."

Nate looked at her uncertainly. "Do you really think you can do it? Kill him, I mean."

Kara shrugged. "Someone has to."

They passed the wrecked fence, clambering over a toppled security tower and into the harbour. The smoke had begun to break ahead of them, eddying on the breeze. Shafts of sunlight cut through and Kara caught a glimpse of something huge and black looming in the fog. The *Kraken*.

Mariner soldiers crouched around the forward

gangplank, firing at a group of Shore Boys who had taken cover in the wreckage of a dockside storehouse. A rocket spiralled up, striking the submarine, but its armour was too thick – the blast left nothing but a charred smear. And the response was immediate; the *Kraken*'s cannons spun, battering the rubble with fire and noise.

"Come on," Kara said, tugging Nate towards the warehouse. "They might know where Joe is."

They crept closer, ducking through shattered walls and around piles of debris. Suddenly a figure stepped from the shadows clutching a rifle.

Kara put up her hands. "We're friends. I'm looking for Maura Glass."

"Kara?" The young man lowered his gun. His hair was flat with grime but Kara felt her stomach roll over as the Pompadour beamed at her. "Mrs Glass hoped you would come. As did I. Your speech was very powerful."

Kara blushed. "Thanks."

"You two know each other?" Nate asked suspiciously.

Kara shook her head. "A bit."

The sun cast long shadows through the demolished storehouse. Groups of people sheltered behind heaps of wreckage, their weapons braced. Kara saw a shock of red hair bright against the grey. Miss Ella held her rifle tight as it kicked beneath her, sending a Mariner soldier spinning into the dust. She nodded to the girl beside her, a long-limbed figure in the tattered remnants of a pastel-green balloon dress.

"Wow," Kara muttered to herself. "It's like everyone we know is here." But remembering Joe's words only made her miss him more.

Maura's eyes shone as she strode towards them, keeping low. "Kara," she said. "Your speech was remarkable. I was so proud. So was Joe."

"Where is he?" Kara asked. "How did Cortez get hold of him?"

Maura flushed. "We can discuss that later. Our scouts report that he's still on the sub, but we can't get any closer. Their defences are too robust; every time we try to advance they blast us."

"I might be able to help," Nate said. "I might know how to take down the *Kraken*."

Kara looked at him. "Really?"

He drew the computer tablet from his jacket; it was dirty and cracked but the screen lit up when he hit the switch. "We're close enough that I should be able to tap into the submarine's databanks … there." He held the device up and Kara saw an interior map of the sub outlined in black. "The engineering schematics are classified, but this shows you where all the important bits are."

"That's great," she said. "But how does it help if we're stuck out here?"

"I'm getting to that. Look, these are the fuel cells, right below the engine. Hit them and the whole thing's disabled. And there's an access hatch just here; it's sealed, but if everyone concentrated their fire on it, grenades and rockets and everything, you might be able to blow it open."

"We've got plenty of grenades," Maura said. "But how do we get close enough without them killing us?"

"You need a distraction," Kara said. "Me and Nate can take care of it."

The Mariner boy sighed. "How did I know you were going to say that?"

27

The Kraken

Kara squared her jaw as they strode towards the *Kraken*, trying to mask the fear running like cold acid in her veins. Her throat was dry, her bare feet were scraped raw and her ridiculous peach dress was smeared with blood and grime. She saw dark eyes lifting from their rifle scopes, the submarine's rocket banks taking steady aim. A squad of Mariners moved to intercept them, others emerging from the rubble. So far the distraction was working.

"The indestructible girl," a familiar voice said. "Cortez knew you wouldn't let us down."

Redeye stepped from the smoke, his sealskin coat in tatters. His face was paler than ever, and Kara could see the strain in his eyes as he forced a smile. *He's scared,* she realised. *Scared they're going to lose. Scared Cortez isn't as all-powerful as he's always believed.*

"I've come for Joe," she said. "Where is he?"

"He's safe," Redeye replied, gesturing. "I'll take you to him."

But Kara stood firm. They needed to give Maura more time. "Sorry for ruining your big plan," she said. "I guess Cortez won't get to rule the Shanties after all."

Redeye reacted just as she'd hoped he would, turning back to glare at her. "It was never about *ruling*. You made things difficult, but it won't matter in the end. The Shanties will be ours and everything will be better. You'll see."

"No, I won't," Kara said flatly. "Cortez is going to kill me. You know that, don't you?"

Redeye flinched, unable to hide his discomfort. Strange, Kara thought, after he'd tried so many times to end her life. But was that fair? In fact, he'd had numerous opportunities and never quite taken them. Even in the tunnel he must've known she'd stood a chance. He was an odd one.

She heard shouts in the distance, followed by the flash of rockets. The soldiers began to turn, raising their weapons, but Kara grabbed Redeye's arm, pulling him towards her. "Wait," she said. "I … I want to say … um, something."

Light flared and Redeye's mouth tightened. "What is

this? One last trick?"

Kara smiled apologetically. "Well, you do keep falling for them."

There was a series of muffled pops, like firecrackers in a tin can. Kara dropped, Nate ducking down beside her. Redeye twisted towards the sound, his good eye opening wide as the *Kraken*'s fuel cells erupted, tearing the side from the submarine in a burst of blue fire.

Heat rolled over them and Kara felt her hair singe. She looked up to see the submarine tilting sickeningly then righting itself, the gangplank lifting off the dock and smashing back down. Clouds of steam billowed furiously and there was a scream like a thousand kettles boiling at once.

The explosions faded and Kara started up, pulling Nate towards the sub. Then she heard a moan like a wounded animal and saw a figure crouching in the fog, hands pressed to his face.

"Redeye?" she asked. "Are you—"

Redeye staggered to his feet, hands dropping away. Kara gasped. His artificial eye still blazed, the metal casing undamaged. But the right side of his face had taken the full force of the blast, melting his skin, scorching his hair and destroying his good eye.

"I'm blind!" he howled, flinching as another blast

shook the dock. "I can't see!"

Kara reached for him but he stumbled away, weaving through the rubble and vanishing into the smoke. They heard a last wail of horror, then he was gone.

Kara turned to the sub. Mariners were spilling from the hatchway and down the twisted gangplank, their hair and uniforms smoking. They streamed past, fleeing into the gloom.

Nate peered up uncertainly. "You really want to go in there? Everyone else is running away."

"Joe's up there," Kara said. "We don't have a choice."

Joe grasped the railing of the balcony as the *Kraken* shook, almost throwing him off his feet. Cortez stood with his legs apart, riding the chain of tremors. He was wreathed in steam and infernal light, fires blazing across the submarine below.

"Father," Cane said from the doorway, "please. We have to go."

The quakes subsided and Cortez turned. His eyes were distant, as though he was barely there at all. "Run away?" he said. "Your people are fighting and you want to flee?"

Joe peered down but all he could see were flames and fog. The gunfire seemed to have petered out; he could hear distant shouts and the groan of melting metal.

"No, I just…" Cane struggled. "I don't want you to get hurt."

Cortez sneered. "Real Mariners don't run. We see things through."

"I'm a real Mariner," Cane insisted, tears springing into her eyes. "If you want to stay, we'll stay."

"No!" Joe protested. "Cane, the battle's over. You're right, we need to run. If your father wants to stay, let him."

"Silence!" Cortez roared. "You already took one of my children from me; I won't let you take the other."

"But she'll die," Joe said. "We all will."

"And who's fault will that be?" Cortez spat. "I came here with good intentions. I came to save your stinking Shanties. It was Kara who ruined everything. I should have listened to Redeye and killed you both while I had the chance. I should have … should have…"

An ugly smile spread across his face and his hand dropped to his belt. Slowly he unclipped his holster, drawing out a slender black pistol. He looked at it for a moment, then he held it out to Cane, his hand steady as the submarine shook.

"You say you're a real Mariner." He nodded towards Joe. "Prove it."

Cane took the pistol, looking from her father to Joe. Then realisation crashed in and she staggered, shaking her head. "Daddy, no," she said. "Please don't make me—"

"I gave you an order," Cortez snapped. "I am still your commanding officer."

Cane swallowed and aimed the gun at Joe, her hands trembling violently. He saw terror in her eyes, but to his surprise he felt himself smiling.

"It's OK," he said. "I know you won't do it."

Cane frowned. "How do you know that?"

"Because of your brother," Joe said. "Elroy couldn't kill me. Neither will you."

"Don't you speak about my son," Cortez growled. "Elroy would've stood by me to the end."

"No, he was good," Joe argued. "Remember what he told me? He was sorry."

"Sorry for leaving me," Cortez snarled. "Sorry for dying before we could carry out our plan."

"I don't think that's what he meant. I think he was sorry for everything he'd done before. You made killing people sound easy, but when he came face to face with it he couldn't."

"Cane, shoot him!" Cortez cried, his voice thick with anger and sorrow. "Now!"

"Daddy, no!" Cane screamed. "I can't."

"You're weak!" he roared, stamping his foot. "Everyone

around me is so weak!"

"I'm not," Kara said, and stepped through the doorway.

Cane froze, the gun still pointed at Joe. Cortez's face twisted as he drove his anger down, forcing himself to smile. It didn't reach his eyes; they were as cold and blue as sea ice.

"At last," he said. "I was beginning to think you'd never come."

"Your submarine's sinking," Kara told him. "Your soldiers have run away. Now I'm going to take Joe and leave while there's still time."

"You're not going anywhere," Cortez replied. "I'm going to kill you, and I'm going to enjoy it."

"Don't you touch her," Nate said, emerging from the sub.

Cortez's expression broke, and he almost laughed. "Oh, this is perfect. My favourite traitor." He looked the boy up and down, shaking his head. "I always knew you'd betray us. Your aunt will be so ashamed when she hears how you turned on your own people."

Nate flushed. "She'll be proud of me for standing up to a bully like you."

Cortez growled. Then he reached for Cane, placing a hand on her shoulder. "Good news, daughter. I'm letting you off the hook for young Joe."

Cane sagged with relief, lowering the gun.

"You can shoot the traitor instead. You've always hated him."

Cane turned pale, her mouth working. "But ... but I..."

"Not this again. Shoot him!"

Cortez's face was warped with resentment and bitterness. He's trying to make himself feel strong, Joe realised. Everything's gone to pieces, and this is all he can do.

Cane jerked towards Nate, biting back a sob. The balcony shook and deep below them Joe heard a sound building, a series of dull thumps like a giant's footsteps.

Nate put up his hands. "Cane, listen. If you don't shoot me, I'll do your gutting-room shifts for, like, a year."

She snorted laughter, crying at the same time. The noise grew louder. Cortez squeezed her shoulder. "Do it," he whispered.

Cane squeezed the trigger and Nate flew back, knocked off his feet by the impact. Kara cried out, Cane screamed, and Joe heard the dull thump of a compressed explosion.

Everything turned to fire.

The sub's prow erupted, white-hot hull plates spinning, a jet of searing flame shooting directly upward. Cortez threw himself forward, shoving Cane clear as the balcony was consumed. Kara pulled Joe through the doorway, her arms tight round him, the roar loud in his ears.

Cortez shrieked, his uniform ablaze, his limbs flailing. Cane cried out but Joe held her back, feeling his eyebrows singe. Then the fire subsided and Cortez dropped to the grated steel balcony, kicking and writhing. Joe remembered that day on the Spur, the burning man on the jetty, the start of all this madness. Cortez rolled, then lay still.

Hearing a groan, Joe was amazed to see Nate picking himself up, weaving unsteadily on his feet. He reached under his jacket and drew out his computer tablet; the screen was shattered, a fibreglass pellet flat in the centre. "Wow," he said. "This thing really came in useful after all."

Kara took the gun from Cane, throwing it over the railing. The girl's face was blank, her hands shaking as she stepped on to the balcony, dropping at her father's side. Behind them the Pavilion was a maze of flame, outshining the last red flush on the horizon. The towers were black, the Wall shrouded in grey. The world was blood and smoke.

"He's alive," Cane said, squeezing her father's wrist. "I think he's alive."

Joe looked at her, and didn't know what to say.

Then the sub shook and Nate grabbed the door frame. "We have to leave."

"The whole place is on fire," Kara said. "We'll never make it."

Nate's face fell. "You mean we're stuck here?"

"I've got an idea," Joe said. "It's dangerous, but I think it'll work."

Kara nodded. "Show me."

Joe clambered up on to the railing, steadying himself as the balcony shook. The sub had listed so steeply that he was almost over the water. "A good jump out and I think we can make it."

Kara peered down, her face full of doubt. Below them the sub's cylindrical body glowed with incandescence. "I don't know," she frowned. "This seems a bit crazy, even for you."

He laughed. "You never just trust me," he said, and jumped.

Kara grabbed the railing, biting back a cry. But Joe cleared the hull by several feet, knifing into the water. For a moment the surface was still, reflecting the flames. Then he rose, giving a thumbs up. Kara breathed out, shaking her head in disbelief.

"Nate, you next," she said. The boy began to protest

and she took his arm. "Don't go soft on me, not after all we've been through."

Nate sighed. "I have been pretty brave, haven't I?"

"The bravest," Kara said, helping him up. "Now jump."

He hit the water with a splash, and came up spluttering. Joe took his hand and together they kicked for the sea wall.

"We need to lift him," Cane said, taking Cortez under the arms. "Here, grab his feet."

But Kara shook her head, gesturing over the railing. "He'll never make it. He'll hit the deck."

"Not if we both push," Cane said. "Come on, he'll burn if he stays here."

Kara nodded. "Yes. He will."

Cane looked up slowly. "You told Nate to go first so he couldn't help," she realised. "You knew he'd want to try." She struggled but her father was a dead weight. With a shout of frustration she let him drop. "If you do this you're a murderer."

"I'm a murderer?" Kara asked. "You're the one who shot Nate."

Cane blushed fiercely. "But I... But he..."

"Your father forced you, is that it?" Kara asked. "You're as crazy as he is."

"He's not crazy." Cane took a step forward. "He's a great man."

"And I suppose he's still going to save the world," Kara sneered. "Give me a br—"

Cane's fist slammed into her face.

Kara staggered back, blood pouring from her nose. Flames coiled below them, jets of steam hissing from the hull. She faced the girl, working her fingers, trying to remember the last time she'd been in a real fight. Not like that tussle on the *Neptune*, but the sort of fight where you genuinely didn't know who'd still be standing, or how many eyes they'd have left.

She feinted and dropped, barrelling into Cane at chest height. They slammed into the railing and Kara clawed, trying to drag her down. Cane threw a punch and Kara stumbled back, shaking the pain loose. Then she hunched her shoulders, feeling strength flow into her fists.

The sub trembled and the balcony tipped further, out over open water. Cane stumbled and Kara lunged again, grabbing with both hands. They hit the sloping floor, rolling and kicking. Kara felt Cane's elbow in her face and twisted, slamming her into the steel grating. In her weariness and confusion she could barely tell where she ended and the other girl began; they were like one exhausted body, cursing and writhing on the smoking deck.

She could hear Cane sobbing now, blinded with tears as she lashed out and missed, lashed out and missed. It was time to end this.

Kara grabbed the girl, pulling her to her feet. Summoning the last of her strength she drove her towards the railing, slamming her into it as the *Kraken* shook.

"No," Cane protested weakly as Kara reached down to grab her ankles. "Don't—"

But by then she was already falling, toppling over the railing and into the black water.

Kara turned back, breathing hard. The fire below seemed to have abated, the submarine sinking slowly into the steaming sea. Cortez lay slumped on the steel. His face was scorched and streaked with grime, but with a start Kara noticed that his eyes were open.

"So it's just you and me," he said weakly, spitting blood. "Here, at the end."

"You're going to die," Kara said. "I'm not going to save you."

Cortez nodded. "Good." He dragged himself into a sitting position. "You know, I still don't understand why you did it, Kara. Those city people made your life hell and you just forgave them."

"I did it for the Shanties," she said, climbing on to the

railing. "To prove we aren't all monsters like you."

Cortez laughed but it turned to wet, red coughing. "Everyone's a monster like me. They just don't show it."

"That's what people like you always think. But Joe's not; he never will be. Nate's not, and I don't think Cane is either."

"What about you, though?" Cortez smiled through blistered lips. "You do what needs to be done. They couldn't have left me to die, but you can. Admit it, deep down you're a monster too."

Kara perched, staring down at him. It would be so easy; all she had to do was fall backwards. She knew she could live with it – there'd be moments of regret, perhaps, but most of the time she'd know that what she'd done was right. Then she heard a shout, and raised her head.

Joe was pulling himself on to the harbour wall, turning to haul Nate up behind him. The Mariner boy slipped and Joe laughed, clear and bright like rain in the night-time. After all this, she thought, after everything he's been through, he can still laugh. What would he say when he found out what she'd done? He'd understand, or he'd say he did. But would he ever really forgive her? Would he look at her the same way, knowing she'd left a man to die?

Joe heaved, dragging Nate to safety. And, gritting her teeth, Kara climbed back down.

28

Afterwards

Dawn found them on the steps outside the Zoo, huddled in the shelter of the Wall as sunlight touched the tops of the towers one by one. The *Kraken* lay smoking, its painted mouth grinning up at them. Joe clasped Growly in both hands – the bear's head had got pretty badly singed, leaving a sort of black stump with eyes. But somehow he still gave Joe courage.

It had been a long, strange night. Joe had slept on his feet or in the arms of whoever was carrying him as they were shuttled from the harbour to the makeshift field hospital down by Deepcut Dock, then cleared out to make room for an endless stream of wounded. Sometime in the small hours they'd been led up to the Zoo, finding space among the sleeping children.

And now it was a new day. Down in the Pavilion he

could see people lifting the dead and arranging them on wooden pallets, Mariner and City and Shanty alike. He knew that before long they'd have to go down and help. Could he carry a body? He wasn't sure. But someone had to.

"My people did all this," Nate said bitterly. "I still can't believe it."

"Cortez did it," Kara said. "Not you."

She'd dragged the Mariner captain from the water, handing him to the Shore Boys who had locked him in the Zoo's deepest cell. Cane had followed, unable to meet Kara's eye.

"I wonder what they'll do with him?" Joe wondered, and Kara shrugged.

"Execute him, most likely. If Maura Glass has anything to do with it."

"They shouldn't," Nate said. "They should find the darkest hole they can and throw him in it. Make sure he never sees his precious ocean again."

"Well, he was wrong about one thing," Joe said, pointing. "Things aren't going to go back to how they were. People are working together already. Look."

A crowd had gathered around the canvas hospital; he could see one of the Shore Boys lifting a stretcher, a MetCo officer taking the other end. Miss Ella had assembled a group of bedraggled city folk and was trying to get them organised, waving her arms like she was back in the classroom.

"How long will it last, though?" Kara asked. "They could be at each other's throats again by nightfall. I don't—"

A sudden wail cut through the stillness. It sounded like a foghorn far out in the shipping lanes. Joe squinted, seeing reflected light in the distance. "Is that a ship?"

Nate shielded his eyes. "A tanker? They might not have heard what happened."

The grey shape rolled into the Cut, slicing through the mist still clinging to the water. That high blast sounded again, echoing from the towers on either side. Then down in the harbour someone cried out, "The Mariners! The Mariners are back!"

They jumped up. Joe still had Redeye's binoculars in his pocket; he tugged them out and peered through, seeing waves cresting round a sharp prow, a silver spire gleaming in the sun. The Disc had been packed into the hangars but the outline of the Hub was unmistakable.

Maura marched from the Zoo, a squad of Shore Boys at her back. "Is it them? Are they really back?"

Joe nodded. "It's the *Neptune.*"

She turned to her men. "Round up as many of our

people as you can. We can win this if we—"

"Wait," Kara said. "We should at least find out what they want."

"They're Mariners," Maura spat. "We know what they want."

"But they're not all the same. Nate's proof of that." Suddenly Kara's eyes lit up. "I've got an idea. Find Cane. Bring her to the docks as quick as you can."

Maura frowned. "Cortez's daughter? What can she do?"

"Just trust me."

They ran down the steps, weaving between the craters. As they reached the sea wall Joe heard the *Neptune* cut her engines, an anchor rattling from the hull. On the upper deck he could see figures at the railing.

"This is the Mariner Ark *Neptune*." The voice came through a loudhailer and Joe couldn't help flashing back to last night, to that terrible moment when Cortez had addressed the crowd. But this was a woman's voice, distant but recognisable. "We received an automated distress call. Where is John Cortez?"

Kara fumbled in her pocket, yanking out Remick's transmitter. "Doctor Chandra," she said, her voice crackling from the busted speakers. "Cortez is … not here."

"Is he dead?" the doctor demanded. "What happened? What did you—"

"Just wait," Kara said, glancing back, "there's someone else who wants to speak to you."

Maura strode towards them, shoving Cane ahead of her. The girl looked exhausted, her face flushing as she spotted Joe and Nate. Then she saw the *Neptune* and her fists clenched.

"We need you to talk to them," Kara told her, holding out the transmitter. "You have to convince them to stand down. You're the only one they'll listen to."

Cane looked at her in astonishment. "Why would I do that?"

"Because of what'll happen if you don't," Kara said. "Think. How few people did Cortez leave behind on the *Neptune*? And how few of those are soldiers? They're loyal to him; they'll fight if they feel like there's no other choice. But they'll die, Cane. You can save them."

The girl blanched. "I'm not a traitor."

Kara's face softened. "I know. But you're not a fool either. And I don't think you're a killer, despite everything. You didn't want to shoot Nate, I know that. And he knows it too, don't you?"

Nate frowned, then he nodded slowly.

"Don't make your father's mistake," Kara pleaded.

"It's time to stop fighting and work together."

They faced one another for a long moment, and Joe could see the struggle taking place behind the Mariner girl's eyes. But at last she took the transmitter, raising it reluctantly to her mouth.

"Th-this is Cane Cortez," she said. "My father's been taken prisoner, Doctor Chandra. I don't know how much you knew of his plans, but… Well, they didn't work out."

The doctor peered over the railing. "And what about you? Are they telling you what to say?"

"No," Cane admitted. "I'm speaking for myself. I just… Look, I know how loyal you all were to him. I know everyone on board loved him, but you haven't seen what I've seen. He did terrible things. He killed so many people. But they fought back. And they'll fight again if you force them."

Chandra lowered her transmitter, turning to the other Mariners gathered at the railing. Among them Joe could see a figure in a wheelchair, his blond hair bright in the sunshine.

"So what do you want us to do?" the doctor asked at last. "Just turn round and go?"

Kara reached out, taking the transmitter from Cane's hand. "Actually we'd like you to stay."

Maura began to protest but Kara held up a hand.

"There are wounded people here. They need medicine and blankets. You have food and fuel on board; we'll need those too. Please. Stay and help us."

Chandra turned away, conferring with the others. Joe saw her speaking animatedly, gesturing down at the docks and the Pavilion. He took Kara's hand, enjoying as he always did the sight of his little brown paw clasped in her big rosy-pink one.

"Maybe it's happening," he whispered. "Just like in your speech. Maybe everyone's really going to work together. Maybe we really are going to make the world better."

Kara nodded as the sun topped the Wall, bathing them in clear light.

"Maybe," she said.

Acknowledgements

Ella Diamond Kahn put the wind back in my sails. Kirsty Stansfield expertly steered me and the Mariners through exposition-infested waters. And as ever, Rosie Greatorex is the star by which I set my course.

Special credit is due to Scott Eastlick – the Mariners are your offspring too (we'll call him Nate, if it's a boy). Jensine Eckwall drew the coolest map imaginable, Manuel Šumberac created that dizzying cover and Elisabetta Barbazza wrangled it all together beautifully.

Lauren Fortune and Tilda Johnson got things back on track while Cavan Scott kept me both inspired and in gainful employment, along with Emil Fortune, Sammy Holland, Nick Kyme, David Jenkins, George Mann and many others. Daisy Brown and Kitty Coulson Byng offered enthusiasm and excellent notes, while Alfie Brown, Sarah Huddleston and Steve Huddleston cheered from the sidelines.

I'd be sunk without Sean, Nic and all the other No Sorrows past and present, my Stokey Litfest patrons Liz Vater and Kate Manning and of course Lindsey Bowden, who enables me to live out my teenage dreams once annually at the Twin Peaks UK Festival.

It's taken a long time to get here so there are far too many friends to thank for their support, particularly this past year. You know who you are, I love you all dearly and I'll see you down the Butchers.